DOWN IN THE HOLLER

Down in the Holler

Bridget Riley

Fire & Feast Books

ISBN 979-8-9922008-2-9
ISBN (ebook) 979-8-9922008-3-6

To my husband and my little ones

Contents

Introduction

Several years before this story ever saw the light of day, an abrasive, scientifically-minded psychic detective started nudging my imagination. She resisted every attempt I made to adjust her personality and her story's trajectory, until I finally gave in and realized that she was going to have things her way or no way. Her name was Judith, and she did not take kindly to nonsense.

While I consider myself to be an open-minded skeptic, I have always been fascinated by stories of ghosts, hauntings, apparitions, and other eerie happenings. I also love learning about cold case investigations, particularly when new discoveries are made years or decades after the initial crime lead investigators to uncover the truth. As I started brainstorming and outlining Judith's first mystery, I had the opportunity to combine these two somewhat disparate enthusiasms of mine into a single, cohesive story, which was an unexpected joy.

I was vaguely aware of Substack in the years leading up to *Down in the Holler*'s original serial publication, it was a happy accident that I stumbled upon the small but active corner of Substack in which an amazingly diverse and talented collection of authors publish fiction. I was immediately intrigued, and I started to wonder if my own quietly compiled short stories, and my percolating idea for a series of psychic detective mysteries, might be able to find a home in this online space.

To get my feet under me, I started sharing my backlog of short stories while I tinkered with a fledgling Substack newsletter, and I slowly dug roots into Substack's fiction community. When, in the Spring of 2024, I was ready to begin serializing *Down in the Holler*, I was surprised and delighted by the support I received, and my tiny newsletter started to grow.

I already had many more mysteries brewing for Judith, and the encouragement I received from Substack's fiction community gave me the motivation I needed to go full steam ahead with another story, *Beasts of the Field*, in Autumn of 2024. A third, *Murmurs in the Walls*, is planned to be published serially on Substack during the Spring of 2025. These stories will also become available in print and e-book after their online release.

The opportunity to share Judith and her quirky personality on Substack has completely changed the secret, solitary writing life I led for many years, in which I wrote in the margins of a busy life and rarely showed my work to anyone. Life is even busier now, with a growing, high-energy brood of children, but writing is no longer such a lonely hobby. I have the gift of not only sharing my work but also connecting with people who enjoy the stories as much as I do, and who choose to spend a portion of their day reading words that I wrote. It's an incredible gift for which I'm so, so grateful. When I look at my writing life today compared to two years ago, it is unrecognizable now, with so much more richness and joy.

Thank you so much for opening this book and taking time to dive into this story. Please stay a while and spend some time with Judith. She's prickly, but she grows on you. I know from experience.

Bridget Riley

I

THE DREAM

*M*ist leeches through the mountains like a living thing, pour-ing down undulating hills and entombing the wet-leafed ground, darkened by the clustered trees.

A trickle, the faint rush of a stream tumbling over rocks and tangled roots.

Ahead – a depression in the leaves, a concealed hole. A distur-bance, unnatural in this isolated place.

Wet, damp, hungry soil, grasping for air and light. Long-fallen leaves, a thick, dead carpet, impenetrable as the lid of a cof-fin.

Leaves stir. A nudge, a straining for release.

Rustling. A glint, pale and translucent, faintly purple, peeking between the slick brown leaves. A rough scrabbling.

Closer.

Deathly white fingers burst from the leafy carpet. A hand, palm creased with soil, reaching, grasping –

...

Judith's eyes flew open with electric suddenness. But she didn't jerk upright in bed, wheezing and sweating. Not this time.

She lay there, frowning, covers pulled up to her chin. Drawing long, deliberate breaths through her nose, she waited until her heartbeat slowed from a rabbit's frantic pitter-pat-pitter-pat to a calm, dull thumping. Then, swinging her legs over the side of her bed and sliding into her slippers, she snatched the small notebook from her bedside table.

Mountains. Fog. Stream. Fallen leaves. Hand in the soil.

She scrawled the date in the upper corner, then tugged on a fluffy robe and padded through the dark hallway to the kitchen.

Flipping on the light to chase away the shadowy corners of the quiet house, Judith filled the kettle and plopped a tea bag into a mug. She glanced at the news app on her phone, grimaced, and turned away.

In the news, she might find an answer.

She might see a name, a story. A missing persons report, an Amber alert, a search party.

She might see a name, and the dream would make a twisted kind of sense. She would figure it out sooner or later. She always did.

Couldn't she just, for a few minutes, enjoy tea and buttered toast in peace?

Judith stuck her phone on top of the fridge. Out of sight, out of mind.

...

The sun, with its pale late-winter harshness, bloomed over the kitchen as Judith screwed on her thermos lid over her coffee. Slinging her laptop bag and purse over her shoulder, she was just heading for the door when her phone rang.

Her phone. She'd almost left it. Judith set down her coffee and stood on tiptoe to reach to the top of the fridge.

The number wasn't in her contacts. But it was a Kentucky area code.

Could be spam, she thought, her thumb hovering over the screen.

Or it could be a client. "Hello?"

"Hi." A woman's voice came over the line, and from the first syllable Judith could hear a thick country drawl in her vowels. "Um. Is – is this Judy Temple?"

"Judith Temple."

"Judith. Sorry. My name's Anna May Schneider. I, um, I saw your ad. Online."

"Yes?"

The woman gave a nervous laugh that shifted into a sigh. "This is probably gonna sound crazy."

"I do the initial consultation for free, and I will let you know if I think your case is a good fit for me," Judith said. "After that, readings come with a fee. And if I have to come to you, then you'll pay travel costs as well."

"Oh. Is this the, uh, consultation?"

"Yes."

"Is this a bad time?" Anna May said, faltering. "You sound like you're in a hurry. Should I call back later?"

"No." Judith pressed the bridge of her nose. *Don't be rude.* Her sister made being pleasant look so easy. Why could she never seem to master it? "No, it's fine. I was about to head out the door when you called. But I set my own schedule, so it's – fine."

"Oh. Okay. So do I just…go ahead?"

"Yes. What's the reason for your call?"

"Okay, like I said, this is gonna sound crazy." Anna May gulped a breath of air, and in the long pause that followed, an image of her appeared unbidden in Judith's mind: *Sandy hair in corkscrew curls, fleshy and sturdy as a Michelangelo painting. A cigarette stubbed out nearby. Trying to kick the nicotine habit, but nerves made her slip up this morning, after the dream.*

So here was her answer. It had found her, as it always did.

"You had a dream, didn't you?" Judith sighed. "Tell me if this sounds right: Walking along a mountain path, lots of fog. You see what looks like a hole in the ground covered over by leaves. You look closer, and a hand reaches out toward you."

For several moments, Anna May was silent on the other end. "How did you know that?" Her awkward cheeriness was gone, her voice quiet.

"Because I had the same dream."

"That's –" Anna May took another noisy breath. "I guess Google led me to the right person."

Judith pulled her notebook from her purse, flipped to the most recent page, and scrawled *Confirmed* beside her scribbled dream. Then she sat down at her kitchen table and opened her thermos. She had hoped to get to the co-op early to settle into her rented office. Didn't seem like *early* was going to happen anymore.

Yet, like a weed in a cracked sidewalk, through her chagrin poked a tingle of excitement. "Tell me what you think the dream means."

A thick pause stretched over the line. "It's just – I guess I don't really know how to do this. I've never called a psychic before."

"Just start at the beginning," Judith said.

"The beginnin'?"

"Lots of people have weird dreams. With this particular dream, what made you pick up the phone and call a psychic detective?"

"It was –" Anna May floundered again, her breaths heavy on the other end.

Judith poked her fingernails into the skin of her palm, fighting to hold her tongue. She was not patient by nature. And she had a work deadline to meet. She needed to get the newest version of her project's code to her boss by Friday, and this nervous, slow-talking Kentucky woman was eating into her Wednesday morning.

"I think the dream is from my sister."

"Tell me about your sister," Judith prompted after another pause.

"Well, she – she disappeared years ago."

Okay, a missing persons case. This was nothing new.

"So what makes you think this dream is from her?"

"My sister, her name was Autumn. Autumn Hanson. She was partyin' with some friends one night – this would have been twenty-one years ago this April. They say one minute she was there, the next she wasn't. Which was pretty normal for her. Mama called her a free spirit. Our stepdad said she was irresponsible and flaky. Sometimes she'd disappear for a few days and then show back up, sayin' she'd been stayin' with friends or her boyfriend or somethin'. She was gettin' high; even I knew that. Oxy hit our town real bad around that time."

"Oxy?"

"OxyContin," Anna May said. "You know, the opioid."

"Your sister was an addict?"

"You come up in the hollers, where all the movie theaters are closed down and the closest bowlin' alley is two hours away in Lexington, you'll find most everyone is an addict," Anna May said, a defensive prickle in her voice.

"Oh." Judith shifted in her seat. She knew rural Appalachia had a drug problem. She'd heard the news reports and seen the headlines of essays and think pieces. But the stony reality of Anna May's tone turned Judith's sterile, vague awareness into something cheap and brittle. "So she had a habit of disappearing and getting high. What happened?"

There was a pause, a breath. "She didn't come back. It wasn't until almost a week later that my mama even called the cops. We never saw hide nor hair of her again, never heard a word. She was just gone."

"What do you think happened to her?"

Anna May laughed, her loping voice breaking in a rueful, ragged sound. "I wish I could say I think she ran off somewhere, found a job, met a nice guy. But it's been twenty years. Twenty years without a word. What else could have happened? I know she's dead. Buried somewhere up in the mountains where there are no houses, no roads. If a young girl goes missin' in these parts and doesn't turn back up, that's where she is."

Judith swallowed. "Okay. So you say your sister sent you this dream. What is it that makes you think that?"

"I think – I think she's tryin' to tell me somethin'."

"Like what?"

"If I knew that, I wouldn't be callin' you," Anna May snapped.

Fair enough. A little more blunt than she'd expected from a coal country woman, but Judith could respect the sentiment. It was the sort of thing she herself would have said.

Anna May gave a little gasp. "I'm so sorry. That was rude. I don't normally say things like that, especially to strangers. I guess it just gets me wound up, talkin' about this."

"Not a problem," Judith said. "So what is it that you want me to do?"

That was a little trick she'd learned from an online negotiation class: Don't ask *why* questions. Not *Why did you call me?* That question prompted defensiveness, not answers.

Much better were: *What is it that you want? What is it that you saw?* Neutral questions that led to concrete answers.

That course had done wonders for her conversation skills, which, she had to admit, were in fairly dire need of help. Constance was the chatty, charismatic sister, not Judith. Constance could charm a story out of a rock. Judith could code a computer program to simulate the rock's geologic formation over time or build a wall made of virtual rocks that fit together in a perfect mathematical pattern. Or, as she was now learning, she could have visions of the rock, about who touched it, who brought it to where it was, who hid a body beneath it.

"I want to know what happened to her," Anna May said. "It's been over twenty years; I know she's not comin' back to us. I just – I want some peace for her."

Judith's eyes roved over her kitchen, with its tidy countertop, its shelves that she had organized for maximum efficiency. The silverware in the optimal drawer for easy placement when she needed to empty the dishwasher. The plates, stacked by size and color, in the cabinet near the stove. The spice rack alphabetized. No photos, no plants, no cozy lamp like Constance had in her house.

This dream, this phone call, this rural Kentucky missing persons case – none of it fit into Judith's schedule.

But –

She had a project due on Friday. Almost everyone at the company took time off after a big project. She had plenty of paid leave, and she'd allotted a portion of it for cases like this that might pop up. There was nothing stopping her from taking next week off.

Judith pushed down the bright, sprouting weeds of excitement, intertwined with sharp tendrils of fear, and took a breath. "I have a work project to finish this week, but I can drive to you on Saturday and stay through next week if needed. You said you're two hours from Lexington?"

"That's right. Salt Fork. It's a little mountain town."

"And you want me to do a reading to try to figure out why and how your sister vanished, and where her body is?" Even as they left her mouth, the words tasted bitter on Judith's tongue, but how else was she to say them? Massaging words to make them more palatable was Constance's domain. Judith's domain was precision.

A sniff on the other line, and Anna May's voice, when she spoke, was thick and wet. "Yes, ma'am."

"Okay, well." Judith drummed her fingertips on the kitchen table and bit her lip. There was no way to be delicate about this. "I accept payment up front. PayPal, CashApp, Venmo, whichever you prefer. I'll forward you my information and contract."

With a hasty goodbye, Judith hung up and slung her laptop bag over her shoulder. It was a strange, liminal space, this in-between where she'd been living since her visions started. Judith was a creature of habit – schedules, plans, checklists. But these dreams, visions – whatever they were – didn't fit into her schedule, couldn't be coded. And they weren't always precise, however hard she tried.

Striding over to the dry-erase calendar on her wall, Judith drew a line through the next week, marking off the days with small, tidy letters.

COLD CASE. SALT FORK, KENTUCKY.

II

THE FAMILY

"Drive-through town" was a generous term for the jumble of buildings that made up Salt Fork, Kentucky. The twisting highway, running like a gray river between tumbling green mountains, for miles had been the only sign of human habitation. Then she had rounded a corner, and there, without warning or preamble, was Salt Fork.

Judith's car crept along Main Street, which seemed to be the only street. It stretched along for a few blocks like a gap-toothed mouth, half its buildings empty and in disrepair.

A tiny library, the mural on its outside wall faded and peeling. Abandoned buildings, out-of-business stores. A greasy diner, its gutters overflowing with rotted leaf corpses. Everywhere, *For Lease* signs.

Judith checked her rearview mirror to make sure she wasn't holding anyone up by driving so slowly, but the street behind her was empty. Her hands tingled, a restless sensation creeping into her body, though she couldn't put her finger on why. Slowing the car to a crawl, she peered at the handful of scruffy people milling about the street.

A scowling teenager stomped toward a dingy grocery store, trailing after a harried-looking woman in sweatpants. A man in a baseball cap lit a cigarette and leaned against a dark red pickup truck. Two men in boots and cowboy hats chatted outside a liquor store.

Nothing to see. And nothing concrete enough to record in her notebook. Judith pushed aside the tingly feeling, double checked her GPS, and kept moving.

Judith liked having answers. And this ability – gift, curse, sense, whatever it was – was not in the habit of giving her clear, precise answers. It was accurate, far more accurate than random chance. But it was layered with her own preconceptions, emotions, worldview, mood – a complex web of filters that snatched away certainty. The engineer in her wanted to quantify, isolate, study these sensations, these visions and premonitions. But this gift of hers, if it was a gift, had other ideas.

The address Anna May had given Judith led her off Main Street, past the whitewashed Salt Fork Church of God, and toward a smattering of tumbledown houses.

The Schneider house was decent enough, a compact, two-story home with a sagging roof and vines creeping up its wooden planks. Judith opened her car door to the clamor of raised voices coming from inside the house.

A man and a woman, though she couldn't make out their words. And a third, shrill voice shrieking at them to be quiet.

Tugging her peacoat tighter against the chilly air, Judith made her way up the front walkway, its worn cement infested with scraggly, opportunistic weeds. The voices rose, jumbling over each other in a ragged tug-of-war.

" – so afraid of?"

"Not in my house!"

"It's been twenty years!" Anna May's voice roared, her Kentucky drawl swallowed in rage. "You're not even her father!"

Judith knocked on the front door.

Silence dropped over the house, leaving only the birdsong of early spring and the faint rumble of a car on the distant two-lane highway.

The curtain rustled in the window, and Judith caught a glimpse of a narrow eye before the fabric jerked back into place.

The door creaked open, revealing a gray woman whose skin seemed to hang, deflated, on her angular bones.

Behind the older woman, Judith saw Anna May, just as she had looked on Wednesday, when her image had floated, unbidden, into Judith's mind: sandy curls, sturdy curves. Probably a nicotine patch under her sleeve. But now Anna May's arms were crossed, her lips pressed tight.

A weatherworn man with a belly and a scraggly beard glowered in Judith's direction. Slapping a baseball cap on his head, he stomped out of the room.

The lovely reception she'd been hoping for.

Judith looked back toward the gray-haired woman to introduce herself, but the words died before they had a chance to form.

The woman stared Judith dead in the eyes. Without a smile, without a hello, without a word.

Judith's mind scrambled for the words she'd been about to spew. *Hello. Hi, my name is* – What had she been about to say? She needed to say something. It was a rule of conversation, a custom, a guardrail, to say hello in greeting. Judith liked guardrails, the failsafe paths through the minefield of conversing with strangers.

But this woman just stared, and Judith stared back.

Anna May, her face blotchy with the dregs of fury, stepped forward. "Hi, Miss Temple. I'm Anna May. We spoke on the phone. This is Cindy, my mom."

Cindy dropped her eyes and stepped back to let Judith inside.

Judith held out her hand to Cindy. "Nice to meet you, Mrs. Schneider. I'm Judith Temple."

"Oh, sorry," Anna May said. "She's Cindy Mitchell. Schneider's my married name. My maiden name was Hanson, same as Autumn's." She gave an apologetic shrug, an awkward giggle. "Sorry, lots of different names. Confusin', I know."

"And the man who just left?"

"Rock Mitchell. My stepdad."

"Nice to meet you, Mrs. Mitchell." Judith dropped her hand when Cindy didn't take it. "Well. Might as well get to it. Which room did your sister sleep in when she lived here?"

"Oh, uh –" Anna May faltered, a shrill cheeriness in her voice. "Don't you wanna hear about Autumn first? What we know about that night, and everythin'?"

"No," Judith said. "My data has shown that too much frontloaded information affects the accuracy of my readings. I prefer to do my initial reading with as little bias as possible, and then confirm the validity of my results with the available facts."

"Oh. That sounds…nice, I guess." Anna May retreated toward a narrow staircase. "Um, Autumn's room was up here. My mom and Rock use it for storage now." She started up the staircase. "You want some sweet tea or water or anythin'?"

"No, thank you."

At the top of the stairs, Anna May turned a corner and opened a wooden door pockmarked by nicks and scratches. "Okay. Well, you can, um, make yourself comfortable."

The room was a maze of boxes. Cardboard boxes, plastic bins. Some lids closed tight, others open and spilling out old clothes and junk. An abandoned, dust-covered standing bike sat in one corner, and an old TV shrouded in a yellowed sheet stood in another.

Everything was haphazard, shoved together without even the semblance of a path between the boxes. Claustrophobic and dark, almost suffocating.

Judith set down her purse by the door, closed her eyes, and waited.

Nothing came.

Or, rather, too many things came, so many that no image, no sound, no memory could break through the chatter. It was a low-level hum – a blank, white radio static.

Judith opened her eyes and picked her way through the jumble of boxes toward the lone, grimy window. Perhaps some natural daylight would clear the room.

In the dull sunlight that pushed past the dirty screen, Judith peeked out the window at the thick-limbed beech tree whose bare branches scratched at the outside wall of the house.

She closed her eyes again.

The static was louder, fracturing her concentration, drowning the words and images straining to make themselves known.

"Is there anythin' I can get you?" Anna May's voice broke into Judith's mind. "Anythin' that might help?"

Judith opened her eyes and turned, her lips pursed with the effort to contain her frustration. Silence would help. A little solitary space to work would help.

Cindy, with her droopy, haggard face, stood in the doorway behind Anna May.

"I'll need to try other rooms," Judith said. "Where did your sister like to go? Which room was her favorite?"

"The backyard." The hint of a sad smile caught the corner of Anna May's mouth. "She was an outside girl."

...

The backyard was a mess of muddy holes and patchy grass, with windblown trash scattered against the chain-link fence. But beyond the back gate, the grass sloped up in a short, steep rush – and then forest. Thick trees, the buds on their branches straining toward spring, cast heavy shadows on the earthy forest floor.

"I'd like a few minutes alone," Judith said over her shoulder. "Please."

The screen door creaked, then banged shut as Anna May and Cindy retreated inside.

Judith closed her eyes. The static was fainter now, but still there, lingering along the edge of her perception.

Autumn. Autumn, the girl with the tree outside her window, who preferred the backyard to the warm house. That was already more than Judith preferred to know when she was searching for impressions. Just knowing that – Autumn's free-spirited draw toward the outdoors – could color her perception of what she found, what she received.

Through the static, an image strained. Autumn, opening a window, reaching her foot toward a sturdy branch. It was dark. There was a party across town, a beat-up truck waiting for her down the block.

Eyes still closed, Judith reached into her bag for her notebook, but a creaking sound startled her. She opened her eyes, and the gate that led up the hill into the forest was open, swinging on its hinges.

And there, where before there had been no one, were two little girls.

A jolt, whether from thrill or fright or some mixture of the two, sprang through Judith, and she held her breath, watching.

The smaller one shook her blonde corkscrew curls, crossing stubborn arms over herself as her chin quivered. The dark-haired older one stood outside the swinging gate, a mischievous smile breaking across her face.

"Come on," she whispered, beckoning. "Come *on*."

But the little blonde girl shook her head.

From the corner of her eye, Judith caught movement in the house. She jumped, hand flying to her chest.

Through a crack in the curtains, she could just make out Cindy's red-rimmed eye before the curtains snapped back together.

Judith whirled back toward the gate and the little girls.

The gate was closed.

The yard was empty, save for her.

Judith let out a breath. Good to know the strange, staticky interference hadn't completely blocked her impressions. Not that she'd learned anything she didn't already know.

Judith opened her notebook and jotted down the place and time.

Two small girls, one blonde, one brunette. Playing on swinging gate –

The hair rose on Judith's arms and the back of her neck, a faint current of electricity rolling over her body. Her shoulders tightened. Slowly, she lifted her eyes.

A dark-haired young woman stood before her. Her face looked no more than nineteen, but her eyes were grim and worn and weary. Dirt stains smeared her clothes and darkened her cheekbones. And glistening on her shirt, pooling on her abdomen, was a wet, blooming puddle of scarlet.

Judith's pen hesitated over the paper.

The woman said nothing, did not move, but stared at Judith, shutters closed over whatever meaning lay beneath her eyes. Was she pleading? Or was it a threat, a warning to stay far away from these hills and the secrets they hid?

"Autumn?" Judith murmured.

The woman did not respond, only stared with fixed, unblinking eyes. A chilly breeze rustled the grass, scratching the new twigs of the beech tree against the wooden house. But the woman's hair did not move with the wind.

"What do you want, Autumn?" Judith said. She glanced back at the window of the house, but Cindy's peeping eyes were nowhere to be seen. "What can I do for you?"

Autumn stood in the yard, arms at her sides, the fatal wound seeping beneath her shirt. Without a movement, without a word, she watched Judith.

She was simply there. And then, suddenly, she wasn't. The yard was empty once again. The watchful sensation faded, and Judith's senses returned to their baseline.

Judith sucked in several deep breaths, heavy with the wet, earthy scent of approaching spring. Turning back to her notebook, she frowned in frustration at her shaking hands.

She would have to parse out the categories for the different impressions before adding them to her spreadsheet. The first, seeing Autumn climbing out the window, had been solely within Judith's mind – a typical psychic vision of the past.

The two little girls by the gate were surely a haunting – or Judith's preferred, more neutral term, *place memory*, which didn't bring to mind wispy, vengeful ghosts.

But the third – an apparition, most likely. Apparitions were capable of interacting with the viewer in some way, but the only interaction Judith could attribute to this woman was that hard, unwavering stare, directly into Judith's eyes.

Autumn wanted something, Judith could feel it.

Feelings were vague, and unverifiable. But with enough data points, she might eventually be able to create an accurate model of how her feelings, her impressions, her limited perception, compared to the facts of a case or situation. But she was only in the very early stages of data collection. All she could do for the moment was to keep scrawling psychic impressions and plugging data points into her spreadsheet.

Judith closed her notebook and slipped it back into her purse. Autumn had reached out four times already. Once with the strange, shared dream on Wednesday, once in a vision from her teenage past, once in the place memory by the gate, and again just now, as an apparition. She had reached out, and she wanted something.

Judith bit her lip. Though it might interfere with the clarity of her impressions, it might be time to collect a bit more data on this Autumn Hanson. Time to combine her psychic impressions with good, old-fashioned investigation.

Standing up, she pushed through the noisy screen door and back into the stale air of the house. Anna May and Cindy, hovering in the kitchen, sprang alert.

Anna May edged closer to Judith, a hesitant anxiety in her eyes. "So…um. Did you…see anythin'?"

"I'm willing to take the case, if you're still interested," Judith said, keeping her tone clipped to cover the last, breathy remnant of fear in her voice.

"You will?"

"But," Judith said, "I noticed there's no police station here. I'm assuming, since Salt Fork is unincorporated, that the county sheriff is your law enforcement?"

Anna May nodded. "That's Sheriff Morrissey, up at the county seat in McFerrin. 'Bout thirty minutes from here."

Judith tugged out her phone and searched for McFerrin. "All right, then. Well, I'm going to need to speak to him."

III

THE SHERIFF

Sheriff Tim Morrissey rubbed his hands over his eyes and tried to comb out the dent in his hair left behind by his hat. First he couldn't connect to the internet, and now, with the internet signal as close to full strength as it could get in the middle of nowhere Appalachia, he still couldn't get onto the private network. When Lexington's IT office had said they'd set him up with a laptop, he thought surely they'd *set it up*. But no. They gave him a slip of paper with muddled instructions.

He wanted to do his job. Just his job. But this job required far more time spent sitting in front of a screen than he had expected when he'd run for county sheriff two bright-eyed years ago. Even lying in wait along a winding county road, checking passing cars for speeding, was better than sitting in his tiny office in front of this screen that reduced every criminal record and piece of evidence to bits and bytes.

He ought to call Lexington. It would be the responsible thing to do, the professional thing, just to call the Lexington sheriff's IT specialist and ask for help.

But the prospect of a halting conversation with the waspish IT guy, who made no effort to hide his surprised disdain that someone Tim's age could be so technologically inept, deflated his lungs. Tim Morrissey, the idiot backwoods sheriff who couldn't tell a VPN from the back end of a cow.

Maybe he could give Sheriff Quinn, over in Bayton County, a call. Ask him if he'd made any headway on the fentanyl investigation. Work by proxy was better than no work at all, even if Quinn called him *kid* and cycled through the same three stories in every conversation.

Tim let out a heavy breath and turned his eyes toward the growing collage of photos on his wall. Young faces, most of them – so young. Bored young Kentucky kids killed by poison pills handed out like candy.

It wasn't Oxy that was rural Kentucky's biggest problem anymore, though it still caused plenty of death and heartache. No, it was fentanyl now – deadlier and faster and harder to catch. He could shut down the Oxy pill mills, but that wouldn't stop the high schoolers from dying of fentanyl overdoses at parties.

For a rural sheriff, it was a constant game of catch-up, changing strategies to get dealers behind bars and drugs off the listless streets, always trying not to step on the toes of the FBI or the DEA while falling ten steps behind the people pushing the drugs. One step forward, two miles back.

A sharp rap at his door startled him back to attention. "Come in," he called.

The door swung open, and, like a blast of cold air, a young woman strode into his office.

"You're Sheriff Morrissey." It wasn't a question, was barely a greeting.

Tim stood quickly and shook her outstretched hand.

The woman nodded. "Judith Temple. I want to talk to you about a cold case. Autumn Hanson. Disappeared a little over twenty years ago."

A weary awkwardness tugged at Tim. In coal country, cold cases were piled as deep as the rolling hills. People, many of them young women, vanished, forgotten. Armchair detectives and gung-ho volunteers came and went, hoping to champion a case, to solve a mystery, to win a victory for justice. But there was no winner in a murder case. "I have to be at the courthouse soon, but I guess I have a few minutes."

Not entirely true – he wasn't expected at the courthouse until three. But it wasn't an outright lie; three was was soonish. Tim gestured to the worn chair opposite his desk. "You said twenty years ago? A case that old might not be in our online system yet. Not all the old files have been scanned. Do you have new information to add to the file?"

"The family has asked me to look into the case, and I would like to keep you apprised," she said, her tone as crisp as her blazer. "I'd also like to have your professional cooperation dealing with any new leads that might turn up."

"The family hired you? You're what, a private investigator?"

"That is correct."

Tim leaned forward. He didn't know exactly why, but he felt it, that familiar twinge, the cue that something was off. "What kind of private investigator?"

A minute flash of frustration crossed the woman's almost-impassive face. "I'm a psychic detective."

Tim stifled the laugh that tried to erupt from him and looked more closely at the woman across his desk. Small and neat, put-together if not exactly pretty, her hair and makeup calculated and precise. He would've pegged her as a young businesswoman or a well-dressed engineer, but a whimsical, hand-wavy psychic? No. "You're welcome to take a look at the files, Miss – ?"

"Temple."

"Miss Temple. Unfortunately, I'm dealing with some technical difficulties. I can't go searching for files right at the moment, and Cathy, my clerk, is out sick today. Maybe you can come back another time."

Miss Temple cocked her head. "I'm getting the sense that you're skeptical."

It didn't take a psychic to figure that out.

Tim cleared his throat. "As I said, you're more than welcome to take a look at the files." He made a show of checking the calendar on his wall. "If you're free on Friday, you can come back at –"

She leaned over the desk to glance at his computer. "You're trying to connect to a VPN?"

"Um – yes."

"That's your technical difficulty?"

Words came easily to Tim, always had, but suddenly he fumbled over them, grasping for a legitimate reason that he couldn't follow the instructions that the scowling IT guy claimed were so simple.

She squinted at the instruction sheet. "May I?"

"May you what?"

"Take a look."

"I'm about to give my IT guy a call."

"Psychic detective work is my hobby, sheriff," she said in her pert, clipped voice. "I work full-time as a software developer. I can have this connected in less time than it would take you to get someone on the phone."

A software developer – so he *was* right about her. Sort of.

Tim hesitated. "I can't let you go poking around on my computer. There's private information on that network about victims, families, crimes being investigated. Emails with other counties and government agencies."

"I have no interest in infiltrating your very important and sensitive emails," Miss Temple said. "But I do have expertise you seem to need." Standing, she strode around his desk, sidestepped him, and pulled his keyboard and mouse closer to her.

She clicked through his computer settings and the app that housed the sheriff department's intranet without once glancing at the little sheet of paper he'd been struggling over for twenty minutes. Then she straightened up and stood back. "Username and password."

"How did – ?"

"I'll let you enter those. I figure you don't want me *poking around* on the network."

Tim leaned over to type in his credentials, and Judith picked up the Lexington IT department's paper.

She frowned and shook her head. "It's not your fault, re-ally. These are terrible instructions."

"That's good to hear," Tim said, a smile creeping back into his voice. "I thought I was the one with the problem."

With one click, the Sheriff's department database popped into view on his screen. Tim sat back down in his desk chair. "Wow. Thank you. Really."

"Does that mean you'll find me that file now?"

"Sorry?"

"The file. Autumn Hanson's file. I took care of your tech-nical difficulty, so presumably that frees up some of your time."

A laugh burst from Tim before he could stop it. "Fair enough."

Judith's face didn't lose its stony expression as Tim strode, still chuckling, to the wall of filing cabinets that housed the dozens and dozens of old files still waiting to be scanned into the database.

"It's all public information, so you're welcome to come back and take a look whenever you need to," he said as he opened the *H* drawer.

"Before you pull out Autumn's file, I have another re-quest."

"Yeah?"

"In the past, when I've worked with law enforcement, the officer in charge did a performance test of sorts. To see if my psychic impressions were accurate."

"Okay. And were they?"

"Based on my calculations of the number of total psychic impressions compared to the number that have later been confirmed as accurate, I have an accuracy ratio of approximately 67%. While that is significantly below the 90-95% confidence interval I would prefer, it is still a significant improvement over random chance. And the accuracy of psychic impressions is particularly difficult to quantify due to their sometimes symbolic nature. If I included the more symbolic impressions in my calculations, I am certain that my accuracy ratio would be higher."

"You – uh – absolutely. Sure."

A stilted silence stretched as Judith stared at him.

"Usually," she said, "the officer chooses a few files at random, has me do a reading, and then compares my results with the contents of the file. I find that it helps to build confidence between myself and law enforcement."

"Sure. Yes. Let's do that." Tim rifled through the file cabinets, the drawers creaking open and bumping shut as he collected half a dozen random files.

At least I'll have a story to tell, he thought. *But I sure am glad Cathy's not here to see this.*

Tim opened one of the files and skimmed the summary at the top of the page – DUI, multiple priors, suspect taken into custody.

He raised his eyebrows at Judith.

Unhurried, she closed her eyes.

Tim fiddled with the brittle folder in his hands and smothered the smile threatening to crack across his face. This was like one of those cheesy early-2000s cop shows, where the psychic shows up for one episode, acts kooky, and says one off-handed thing that leads the detectives right to the culprit. Except this story would never get past the kooky psychic bit.

"I'm seeing trees," she said. "At night. And a pickup truck."

Tim glanced down and scanned through more of the details of the report. Sure enough, the driver had been pulled over at 11:29pm out on the country highway between Salt Fork and Potters Well. In a beat-up Ford pickup truck.

"Bottles on the floor, mostly cheap beer." Judith opened her eyes and looked up. "How much of that was accurate?"

Tim cleared his throat. "There are a lot of DUIs out here. Trees are everywhere, and almost everybody has a pickup."

Judith pulled a small notebook from her bag, flipped it open, and started scribbling in it. "So each of those statements was correct?"

"You could say that."

She set the notebook down on his desk and fixed her gaze on him. "Would it give you more peace of mind to do a double blind test?"

"A what?"

"You don't look at the file until after I do my reading. That way you can be sure I didn't somehow sneak a look."

Tim grabbed an empty cardboard box from the corner and dropped the remaining files into it.

"Make sure you select a file first," Judith said. "I don't want to do my reading on the wrong one."

"No, we wouldn't want that," Tim said with a smirk. Shielding the box from Judith's view, he removed one of the files and set it behind the box, out of sight. "All right, I picked one. Do your thing."

Again Judith closed her eyes, and a few minutes ticked awkwardly by.

"A needle," she said. "Blood, a lot of blood, on a sidewalk and grass. Tire marks on the road."

Tim opened the file and did a cursory reading of it. "Well, you're not completely wrong."

"Completely?"

"It was a hit-and-run. Don't know what needles have to do with anything, though."

"Not *needles*, plural. One needle."

"Right. Well, let me get that file for you. Autumn Hanson, was it?"

"I'd like to do at least one more," Judith said. "The more data points we have, the better."

Tim shrugged. "If you like." He pulled another file from the box and tucked it away from the psychic's line of sight.

Judith closed her eyes and sat, longer this time, a crease forming between her eyebrows. "There's a broken clock; the glass of its face is shattered. Thorns. Broken dishes on the floor. A very tall man. Children hiding in the bedroom."

When Tim opened the file, he read a brief, dry description.

"Well?" Judith said.

"Domestic violence call, and sure, there were children in the home at the time," Tim said. "But there's no way to corroborate that you're doing any *woo-woo* psychic stuff."

"'*Woo-woo* psychic stuff?'"

"You could be taking a wild guess with domestic violence and spewing out whatever you'd expect to see in a situation like that."

"But I'm not."

"But that's the whole point of this, isn't it?" Tim said. "To prove something to me. I'm not seeing enough evidence that you're not just getting lucky. I mean, needles, thorns, broken clocks. I'm seeing as many misses as home runs."

A consternated shadow passed over Judith's face. "I've gotten the nature of the report correct on every single one."

"I'd have to do a whole lot more of these tests before I'd be convinced that there's anything supernatural going on here."

"Technically, it's not supernatural. It's paranormal. There's a difference." Judith straightened her blouse. "But this doesn't seem to be a very fruitful line of conversation. If you wouldn't mind getting me that file, I'll take a look at it and be on my way."

...

From his desk, where he sat using his now perfectly-functioning VPN, Tim looked up occasionally at Judith, scribbling notes in the corner as she thumbed through Autumn Hanson's file.

A sticky, shameful knot twisted in his stomach. There was something about this woman – he couldn't write her off quite as easily as he'd expected. Her guesses, and her misses, had been just close enough to give him a faint, nagging doubt.

But no, it was luck. She'd gotten lucky.

Or she was trying to con him.

Even as the thought crossed his mind, Tim's own memories popped up to challenge it.

She had asked him to test her. *She* had suggested that he pick random files, that he hide them from her, that he do a double-blind test to prevent himself from unwittingly giving away clues. Every step of the way, she'd been pushing for more transparency, not less.

No, it wasn't a con. Just dumb luck.

Glancing up to make sure Judith wasn't watching him, Tim pulled the files, which he'd left splayed across his desk, closer to him.

The first file – that had been eerily correct, down to the time of day. But really, most DUIs out here in the middle of nowhere happened at night, when people were heading home after an evening of drinking. Nothing too amazing about a DUI at night.

Moving on to the second file, the hit-and-run, he read through it more carefully this time, noting that the victim had been on the sidewalk at the time. Blood on the sidewalk, just as she'd said. And tire marks.

Then his eyes caught something they hadn't before.

At the time of his death, the victim had been high on meth, a pinprick in his arm.

EMTs had found a dirty needle in his pocket.

Tim sucked in his breath and snatched the third file.

On the first page was the report of the domestic violence call – nothing about a clock or dishes, though the officer noted that the house was in bad shape and plenty of things were broken or out of place.

On the second page, which Tim hadn't even bothered to check before, was a mugshot of the husband.

He was a big man, his head smooth as a bowling ball and his beard unkempt and long as though trying to make up for the lack of hair above. With glazed eyes, he frowned at the camera, his hambone arms clutching the placard inscribed with his name and the date.

His arms –

Tim's heart pounded so hard he could hear it in his ears.

Up the man's arms wound tattoos – intricate, interwoven designs, winding like veins from his wrist to his shoulder, all held together by twisted thorns.

Thorns. All over this man, the perpetrator.

Suddenly cold and breathless, Tim leaned back in his chair.

One by one, each of these were strange coincidences. He could call them lucky. He could shrug them off.

But all of these guesses, from one woman, in one test of random samples?

Judith suddenly stood, startling Tim from his thoughts.

"Here's the file back," she said, dropping it on his desk. "I won't take up any more of your time."

She started for the door, and Tim lurched to his feet. "Miss Temple?"

Judith paused and turned, her hand on the door and an irritated tightness in her mouth.

"I need you to see this." Tim held out the third file, opened to the mugshot of the tattooed man. "I owe you an apology."

She blinked, the wariness slipping from her face. "Oh."

"If you have a few minutes," Tim said, "maybe we can talk a little more about this Autumn Hanson case."

IV

THE WITNESSES

It was a case of tunnel vision, pure and simple.

Whoever had been sheriff of McFerrin County twenty years ago had hung his investigation on Autumn's then-boyfriend, Granger Combs, to the exclusion of everyone else in and around Salt Fork.

Statistically the boyfriend was a likely suspect. But there was another candidate who apparently had never been investigated by any authorities, local or federal, and, from a statistical standpoint, was just as suspicious.

Rock Mitchell. The stepfather.

Judith raised her hand to knock on the front door of the Mitchell house, where today the only yelling came from the noisy television inside.

"Judith!" came a voice behind her.

Judith whirled around toward the quiet street to see Anna May leaning out the window of a minivan.

"You talkin' to my mama and stepdad this morning?" Anna May bellowed into the chilly air.

Judith hesitated on the front porch. Yelling across lawns was not her preferred method of communication. She could move closer to Anna May and eliminate the need for hollering loudly enough to alert half the neighborhood. But if she walked to the street to talk to Anna May, Rock and Cindy might open the door. And every moment she spent stumbling back through the muddy yard toward the house was another moment they could slam the door in her face and refuse to speak to her.

Judith kept her feet rooted to the porch. "That was my plan."

"What?"

"That was my plan," Judith said again, the loudness of her voice awkward and strained.

"Let me go in with you!" Anna May's car jerked forward, and she swerved into the driveway. Extricating herself from the van, she stuck her head back in through the window. "Two minutes, Jason. I'm leavin' the keys 'cause it's cold, but don't you even think about climbin' up in the front seat or lockin' the doors while I'm gone."

In the car, a lanky, dark-haired boy sat with his head bent over a phone and didn't even look up in response.

"Now, Judith, you still have that list I gave you, right? Of Autumn's friends back in the day? Most of 'em still live in town." Anna May strode past Judith, collected a spare key from beneath a garden gnome, and unlocked the door. "Knock knock!"

As Anna May and Judith stepped inside, Cindy popped her head around the corner. When her haggard eyes caught sight of Judith, she retreated into the kitchen.

"Don't count as knockin' if you've already opened the door when you say it." His back to them, Rock Mitchell nursed a cup of coffee in front of the massive, blaring living room TV. When he glanced their way and spotted Judith, his face soured. "I told you, I ain't gon' talk to no con woman. You're wastin' your money."

Judith raised her voice over the TV. "Where were you on the night Autumn disappeared, Mr. Mitchell?"

Anna May's eyes widened. "Oh jeepers."

Rock turned around in his seat, squaring himself with Judith. "What'd you just say to me?"

Anna May stepped backward toward the door. "I gotta take Jason to school. I'll – um – call you later today, Judith. Bye, Rock. Love you, Mom."

The screen door slapped shut behind her.

"I asked you where you were on the night Autumn disappeared," Judith said.

Rock jabbed at the remote, and the TV went black and silent. "I ain't gon' listen to this." With a grunt, he hauled himself to his feet and started for the kitchen. "I'd throw you outta my house if I wasn't leavin' for work anyway."

He swung his mug into the kitchen sink with a clatter that made Cindy jump, then snatched his baseball cap and coat from a hook.

Turning back to Judith, he glowered at her from under the low rim of his hat. "I better not catch you in my house again, ya hear me? Go bother somebody else's family."

He slammed the door, rattling the pictures on the wall. Outside, his footsteps crunched across the winter-dry grass, and then his beat-up pickup truck rumbled to life.

Judith took another step into the small kitchen, with its faded linoleum floors and yellowish wallpaper. "Mrs. Mitchell, perhaps you remember where Mr. Mitchell was that night. Was he with you?"

"Why're you here, huh?" Cindy snapped. Judith realized with a jolt that it was the first time she'd heard her speak.

"Anna May hired me," Judith said.

"To do what? Dredge up the past? It's been twenty years. You ain't gon' bring my baby back, so what're you tryin' to do?"

"Based on what I've learned from Anna May, my own psychic impressions, and Autumn's case file, I have two objectives," Judith said. "I want to figure out what happened to Autumn –"

And locate her body. The dark-haired, stony-eyed apparition of two days before, her abdomen puddled with glistening blood, her face and clothes smeared with dirt, sprang from Judith's memories. Anything less than blunt honesty tugged and pinched at Judith like too-tight clothes. But even she knew that describing to a victim's mother the precise state of her child's ghostly apparition would do more harm than good. She'd eventually have to state the facts as she understood them – that Autumn was dead, buried somewhere up in the endless mountain hollers – but perhaps today wasn't the day.

"And what?" Her gray hair hanging over her shoulders in limp curls, Cindy crossed her arms and narrowed her eyes. "What's your second objective, miss psychic lady?"

"And –" Judith hesitated. "Just one. I miscounted. I have one objective."

Cindy scoffed and returned to scrubbing dishes in the sink.

What did Cindy know? Did she suspect her husband, or know where he had been that night? Why was she so averse to Judith's services? Many families would jump at any possibility of finding their missing loved ones – why not her?

Taking a quiet step back, Judith closed her eyes and focused on Cindy.

Judith waited, listening. Reaching out into the world in a way that she didn't fully understand and couldn't quantify – looking for anything, any impressions clinging to Cindy, any echoes of her memories and grief.

But there was nothing. No image came to Judith, no vision of the past, no lingering memories. There was only noise. Only that same, persistent static, like a crossed radio signal. She couldn't pick up anything.

There was something about this house, a strange interference every time she tried to use her abilities. Scowling in frustration, Judith opened her eyes.

Cindy, soap bubbles dripping from her wrists, stared at Judith. "What the Sam Hill you doin'?"

Judith cleared her throat. "My job."

"Get outta my house. And don't you even think of comin' back here."

...

"Salt Fork doesn't have a single place that makes lattes?" Judith peered into the greasy cup of coffee in front of her.

"We got one street in this town," Granger Combs said, a half-cocked smile on his face. "Rudy's Diner's the closest thing we got to a coffee shop."

Judith took a sip, frowned, and shook a packet of powdered creamer into the cup. She stirred it clockwise, clinking the spoon against the cup, breaking up every clump of powder until the coffee turned from black to a muddy river brown. She tasted the coffee again, then looked back up at the trio watching her from across the booth. "As I mentioned on the phone, I'd like to take a few minutes to do a psychic reading on each of you before we begin."

"Little weird, but okay." Granger grinned and slung his arm around the blonde woman beside him. The narrow-faced man on Granger's other side tucked his hands into his lap and studied the water rings on the cheap laminate table-top.

Closing her eyes, Judith pushed away the awkwardness of the sudden silence.

She focused first on the blonde woman, Melissa Sloan, an old friend of Autumn's. Melissa would have been a beautiful woman if she'd been born with a little more money, a little more of a chance in life. But, nearing forty, her skin was sallow and flaky from decades of cigarettes, harsh soap, and poor nutrition. That was what slipped into Judith's consciousness: stunted growth, claustrophobic horizons. Flower petals withering, floating away on a rough gale of mountain wind.

And a baby.

Judith opened her eyes. Melissa stared back, wide eyed.

Don't bring up pregnancies unless the woman says something first, Constance's voice echoed in Judith's mind. Judith had flouted that rule before, and it never ended well.

Closing her eyes again, she focused on Granger Combs, a lean man with car oil on his hands and the lingering remnants of an athlete's physique.

"We allowed to talk while you do your thing?" he said.

Judith kept her eyes closed. "I'd prefer if you wait until I finish."

"Just don't want nobody to think you're sleepin' and we're all just sittin' here starin' at you."

Judith ignored him.

Cars overhead, tools in a box, just within reach –

Granger's voice came again. "Mel, you gettin' the sliders?"

The images stuttered in Judith's mind. *Granger and Melissa, empty beer cans by the trash bin, an argument –*

"What 'bout you, Stewart? Myself, I'm gettin' the bacon burger."

"Mr. Combs," Judith snapped. "You're being very distracting."

"Sorry." He smiled his disarming, lopsided grin. "Don't you wanna get to know us first? Wouldn't that help with your readin's, or whatever you call 'em?"

"No." Judith closed her eyes and started again.

She waited, reaching out into the ether.

Her concentration broken, the images retreated into nothingness.

Judith pursed her lips and stifled a huff of frustration. She'd have to try Granger again later.

She turned her focus to wiry, nervous Stewart, with his persistent cough.

For a few moments, it seemed as though the images wouldn't come, as if they'd all been chased away. But then, like sparks suddenly caught by a gust of air, they flickered to life.

A tunnel, low and dark, with electric lights running overhead. The whir and crash of machinery scraping rock. Dust, thick and heavy, settling on everything – machines, skin, clothes, faces.

But something else nagged at Judith. Not a vision she could see, but a sensation. A hungry pit of suspicion and shame, a heavy burden.

Stewart had a secret.

...

Though questions itched under the surface of her skin, Judith waited for two minutes after the food arrived, letting Melissa, Granger, and Stewart start into their lunches.

Then, when the questions threatened to claw their way out of her, she leaned across the table toward Granger.

You picked up Autumn in your truck the night she disappeared." Judith eyed Granger as he devoured his bacon burger like a starving man. "Where were you going?"

Granger spoke around a mouthful of food. "Party at Stewart's house, I think. It was a long time ago."

"It was the last time you saw your friend alive," Judith said. "Surely it left some sort of impression."

"Well, sure. But some of the things we were doin' that night don't really help you form memories, if you know what I'm sayin'."

"I assume you mean drugs."

"We were in high school, ya know. Not a lot to do up here."

Granger's grin never wavered, but Melissa picked at her food while Stewart shifted in his seat.

"The party was at your house?" Judith watched Stewart closely, but he didn't meet her eyes.

"For a bit," Stewart said. "Then we headed out to someplace else."

"Someplace else?"

The clinking coffee cups of the diner's few other patrons punctuated the silence.

"Where was this *someplace else*?" Judith said.

"Somebody's old family hunting cabin, I think." Melissa dunked a french fry in ketchup, then dragged the fry around her plate, leaving a wet, red ring circling her food. "Not one of our friends. It was somebody from another town. We just followed the directions until we found everybody's cars parked up in the mountains."

"Would you be able to find this cabin again?"

Melissa shook her head. "I ain't been there since."

"What about the two of you?" Judith turned to Granger and Stewart.

"They were selling hard stuff up there," Granger said through a mammoth bite of food. "Harder'n you could usually get in town back then."

"Are you saying you don't remember?"

"We're saying it was a long time ago," Stewart said in his thick, quiet voice.

"What happened to Autumn at the party?"

"Don't remember much," Melissa said. "She always kinda did her own thing. Sometimes she sat and talked to people, but if she wasn't in the mood, she might take a walk or go out on the roof or dance on the table, or anythin', really."

"She was there one minute and gone the next?"

"I'm just sayin' I don't remember. I came back that night with Stewart and Granger, and she wasn't with us."

"What time did you come back?"

"I don't know," Melissa said. "Probably 'round four in the mornin' or somethin'. That was pretty normal for us on a Saturday."

Granger swallowed his food with a noisy gulp. "We looked for her, though. Looked all around the house and a little bit in the woods before we headed back."

"You left her with no ride home from a cabin somewhere in the woods?" Judith raised her eyebrows.

"You gotta understand," Granger said, "Autumn did stuff like this all the time, disappearin' without tellin' nobody where she was goin'. This wasn't nothin' unusual."

"So you didn't think anything of it? Didn't try to look for her the next day?"

"Not until 'bout a week later, when her mama started callin' around to people's houses lookin' for her. Sheriff treated it like a runaway case for a while, then eventually they started lookin' for witnesses, askin' 'bout a body and such. But never found nothin', far as I know."

Judith stared hard at Granger's face, a daub of mustard in the corner of his mouth. "You were Autumn's boyfriend, weren't you?"

Granger leaned back in his seat and let out a long, heavy breath. "Off and on."

"At the time she disappeared, were you off or on?"

"Don't really remember. Hard to know with Autumn."

"You were on," said Melissa.

Granger's smile returned, and he pulled Melissa closer, his arm around her shoulders. "You remember better'n I do. You were jealous even then." He winked at Judith.

Judith leaned in and lowered her voice. "What kind of a relationship did Autumn have with her stepfather? Rock Mitchell."

"They could not *stand* each other," Melissa said, her bland voice suddenly animated. "At each other's throats all the time, lots of shouting matches. He was a hard line kinda guy, and there wasn't no way you could fence Autumn in for more'n two minutes."

"Do you think it's possible that he could have had something to do with her disappearance?"

A silence, thick as the gravy that slopped over Judith's untouched biscuits, filled the air around the table.

"Stewart, you've been awfully quiet," Judith said.

Stewart shook his head. "I don't know nothin' 'bout Rock Mitchell. Hardly ever said two words to him."

"Did you see Autumn leave that night?"

"What?" Stewart hesitated. "No. Look, I gotta go."

Standing, Stewart tossed a ten-dollar bill on the table. "Gotta pick up my wife from the hospital."

Judith frowned. "The hospital?"

"She works there," Stewart said, scooting out of the booth. "Respiratory therapist."

"Stewart makes his hard-earned money down in the mines so he can pay his wife to treat him when he gets coal lung." Granger smiled, clapping Stewart on the back.

Without another word, Stewart turned, made his way through the tiny diner, and pushed through the door.

Judith slid from her seat and darted after him.

Shoving open the heavy front door of the diner, she caught up to him on the sidewalk. "Stewart, just a minute."

He stiffened and turned back toward her.

Judith lowered her voice to a whisper. "I know you're keeping a secret of some kind. Is it about Autumn?"

"I don't know what you're talkin' 'bout."

"I'm not accusing you of anything. But if you know something that might help –"

"You're off your rocker, lady." He strode to his car, parked along the nearly empty street.

"Just take my card." Judith pushed the little piece of cardstock at him. "In case you change your mind."

Scowling, Stewart snatched it from her hand, shoved it in his pocket, and slammed his car door.

...

While the daylight faded to a chilly pink and the sun sank below the dark green mountains outside her window, Judith sat at the cramped desk in her room in McFerrin, the only town within an hour radius that was big enough to host a motel, and scrolled through the few old Salt Fork news articles available online.

Judith had spent the day driving from house to house, talking to Autumn's old friends and classmates, asking the same questions and getting psychic impressions of the same unrelated small-town dramas – gossip, dysfunctional families, the ever-present specters of Oxy and fentanyl. Nothing that helped Autumn's case.

Twenty intervening years was enough time to make a case very, very cold. But cases had been solved after longer lapses, and Judith suspected that at least *someone* in this tiny mountain town knew what had happened to Autumn Hanson.

In a town that seemed too small for secrets, this one unsolved crime gaped, a black hole in the middle of the tiny community.

Judith's phone rang, making her jump.

An unidentified Kentucky number.

She snatched it on the second ring. "Judith Temple."

"I changed my mind." The voice spoke in little more than a whisper, barely audible over the noise of a TV in the background.

"Stewart Mullins, I presume?"

"How'd you know that? You see a vision of me callin' or somethin'?"

"On occasion I have been known to use basic human reasoning skills. I knew you were lying and wanted to come clean, and I gave you my card," Judith said, letting the statement linger. "And I also recognized your voice."

"I ain't –" he started, his voice rising. Then, with a sigh, he lowered it back to a whisper. "I ain't lyin' 'bout Autumn. I didn't do nothin' to her, and I don't know where she is."

"Then what are you hiding?"

Stewart took a breath, and all Judith could hear on the other line was the television behind him.

"Stewart?" she said.

"I found a note."

"A note?"

"Autumn left it at the cabin, on one of the beds, that night she disappeared. For Granger, I guess, but I don't know if he ever saw it. Maybe he did. I don't know."

"What did it say?"

Stewart paused again. "You want a picture of it?"

"What do you mean a picture? You kept it?"

"I – yeah, I kept it."

Then, without even reaching out for it, Judith saw him.

Stewart, skinny and pimply and shy. Always sidelined, always tagging along. Always Melissa's date, both of them watching with starving eyes as Granger and Autumn did their push-and-pull, dating and breaking up again and again like a broken record.

Then, one night – a note on the bed. A note for the boy who would never care about Autumn like Stewart did.

He snatched the note, tucked it away in his pocket.

The vision cleared, and Judith saw only her dingy motel room and the rosy sunset.

Lovesick, awkward Stewart had stolen the note, hidden it away all those years ago. The small, petty act of a jealous teenage boy.

But then Autumn never came back.

And the note, potential evidence, had festered in Stewart's mind, burning his peace, a hot ember hidden in the ash of a long-dead fire.

Judith's phone dinged.

Jerked from her thoughts, she moved her phone away from her ear and clicked on the message.

It was a photo taken from a phone camera. On a kitchen countertop sat a wrinkled, yellowed note on lined notebook paper, faded letters scrawled in an untidy hand:

Follow me if you care.

V

THE RED HERRING

Bundled up against the chilly morning, Judith sat in her car in the parking lot and stared at the photo on her phone.

Follow me if you care.

Vague, calculated to induce guilt and pity. It had all the hallmarks of an insecure teenage girl grasping at attention.

The note seemed old, at least from the photo. And her vision last night had confirmed Stewart's story of finding the note and taking it in a petty act of teenage jealousy. Apparently holding onto it in secret for two decades, the last remnant of the vanished girl with whom he'd been infatuated.

But Judith knew, though it irked her, that her visions didn't always tell the full story. There were layers, too many for her to quantify. Layers of her own biases, of the subject's perception of events, of other, unknown factors working behind the scenes.

Stewart likely had found the note, just as he'd said. But how was she to know Autumn had written it?

Or what if, after finding the note, Stewart had followed Autumn been rebuffed, and killed her in a moment of jealous rage?

And what had changed Stewart's mind about coming clean yesterday? Had he thought she would eliminate him as a suspect if he gave her just enough of the truth to placate her?

Judith zoomed in on the photo of the note again.

Follow me if you care.

If Granger had seen this note, if he'd followed her into the woods or wherever she'd gone...

Judith's stomach tightened at the thought of grinning, bacon burger-eating Granger, law enforcement's pet suspect, stalking into the woods after his on-and-off girlfriend, but she pushed the sensation away. She just needed a solid breakfast, and her clenching stomach would settle. She would be objective, however much her stomach tried to sway her otherwise.

A pickup truck pulled into the parking lot, and Judith looked up in time to see Sheriff Morrissey, with his hill country cowboy hat, climb out and start moseying toward the door of his office.

Judith opened her car door to a rush of cold, damp air. "Sheriff!"

Tim blinked in surprise as he unlocked the door. "Miss Temple! Good morning."

"You can call me Judith."

"And you can call me Sheriff," he said with a quirked smile.

Judith caught up to him at the door, which he held open as she strode into the dark office. "I have some potential evidence, but I'll need a handwriting expert."

"We don't have one of those in this county." Tim turned on the lights, and the stark, yellow-green light hurt Judith's eyes after the gentle sunrise outside. "I can check with Lexington, though, if the lead seems promising enough."

"It's promising." Judith pulled up the photo and handed her phone to Tim. "Last night Stewart Mullins sent me this. He claims that he found it the night Autumn disappeared, that she left it for Granger Combs, her boyfriend."

"We'll need a handwriting sample for comparison. You know if Autumn had a diary or anything? The longer the sample, the better."

"I can ask."

Tim frowned at the photo. "Does Stewart know if Granger saw the note?"

"No." Judith squinted at the sheriff. Tone of voice and micro-expressions, the little cues that her sister Constance could read like a second language, often went over Judith's head, but even she heard the change in the sheriff's voice. "Do you know Granger?"

"Seen him a few times. Know him by reputation more than anything. Not a great guy, from what I understand."

"He was very friendly and open when I met him."

"Maybe so," Tim said. "But he's done some time for dealing Oxy, and the sheriff before me said he got called to

Granger's house once or twice to break up shouting matches between him and his girlfriend."

"Oh." Judith took her phone back and slipped it into her purse. "Not to discount the seriousness of his jail time, but I understand that a high percentage of the population in this area is addicted to opioids."

Tim sighed. Pulling off his hat and dropping it onto his desk, he ran a hand through his hair, indented from the band of his hat. "Most everybody has at least one addict in the family."

Judith's eyes darted to the wall beside Tim's desk, where a collage of photographs hung on a bulletin board. Faces, so many of them young. Some of them barely more than children.

No vision came to Judith's mind, but a sudden sadness settled on her shoulders, a weight threatening to press her down through the floor, through the concrete, into the coal-rich mountain earth.

Judith grabbed the edge of the sheriff's desk, trying to suck in a breath against the weight crushing her lungs.

"You okay?" Tim's voice broke through the strange, muffled silence, and the weight was gone as suddenly as it had appeared.

Judith breathed, her lungs again stretching to their full capacity. "I'm fine."

The door swung open with the jingle of a bell, and a woman with a soft, grandmotherly body and sharp eyes entered the small office.

"Mornin', Sheriff," she said, aiming a hospitable smile at Judith. "Pesky virus is all gone, so you're stuck with me again. Looks like you're startin' early."

"Cathy, this is Judith Temple," Tim said.

"That psycho who's been drivin' all over the county lookin' for that girl from Salt Fork?" Cathy looked over her glasses at Judith. "You don't look like a psycho."

"*Psychic*," Judith said. "*Psycho* means something completely different."

"Oh, it does?" Cathy unpacked her bag and ensconced herself at her desk. "Silly old me."

...

Judith preferred not to let apprehension, her own or other people's, be a barrier to the truth. But even so, an anxious discomfort prickled her skin as she stepped into Fix 'Em Roy's Car Repair Shop and made her way to the garage.

"Granger Combs?" she said to the cluttered room, filled with the tinny, acidic scent of old metal, rust, and engine oil. "Granger?"

"Over here."

Judith followed the voice through the room, past cars in various states of brokenness, and up to a rusty pickup truck hoisted on a jack and lever. Granger wheeled himself out from beneath it and sat up.

"Psychic lady! What brings you out this fine day?"

"This." Her stomach twisted, but Judith held out her phone.

Frowning, Granger stared at it. "What's this?"

"It's a note that Autumn wrote the night she disappeared."

"Whoa. You're sure?"

Judith hesitated a fraction of a second. Was she sure? She hadn't actually seen the note in person, and Tim hadn't heard back yet from Lexington about a handwriting expert. No, she wasn't sure at all. But she needed to know if this easy-talking, Oxy-dealing, small-town mechanic was capable of murdering Autumn. If he was responsible for the dirt-smeared, bloodstained woman who had appeared in the backyard of the Miller house.

"I have reasonable certainty, yes," Judith said, crossing her arms.

"It sounds like something she woulda wrote." Granger placed his wrench into the meticulously-organized toolbox beside him and pulled out pliers. "How's this note poppin' up outta nowhere after twenty-odd years, though?"

Judith twitched at Granger's verb conjugation, but, taking a deep breath, she decided not to address it. "Someone has come forward."

Granger held Judith's gaze, and her fingertips began to tingle with an uncomfortable, vulnerable sensation, as though her face were a window, transparent and brittle.

He shook his head. "Stewart was always sweet on her."

"I've talked to many, many people in Salt Fork over the past three days –"

"You gonna try to tell me it's not Stewart? What'd he say? That he thinks I killed her? All these years, sittin' in my house, drinkin' my beer, and the whole time he's been thinkin' I'm a murderer?" Granger chucked the pliers into his toolbox with a clatter and stood up, striding away from Judith, his fingers combing and clutching his hair. He turned back toward her. "She ran away all the time. Anybody tell you that? She'd be here one day and gone the next, doin' drugs with whoever would sell 'em to her. She dropped outta school in eleventh grade, never once held down a job, and slept on other people's couches whenever Rock kicked her out for not earnin' her keep. She was in with all kinds of people, bad people. But when she went missin', everybody looked at me. Even you. You been in this town three days, an' I'm your number one suspect."

Granger's face splotched red, but Judith held her ground, her arms crossed and her face impassive.

"Actually, you're my number two suspect. I find Rock Mitchell to be highly suspicious."

Granger's shoulders crumpled in a breathy, rueful laugh. "Well, that's good to hear, I guess."

A sheen sprang into his eyes. Judith shifted on her feet, biting her lip. Why would anyone cry in front of a relative stranger? She could not imagine anything more humiliating. There was no possible way for such behavior not to be awkward for both parties. And yet not only did Granger stay beside her despite his leaking eyes, but she could detect no physical signs of embarrassment in his body language. Judith studied her shoes, waiting for him to stop.

Granger spoke again, his voice thick. "I kept thinkin' she'd come back. Thought she'd just hopped a bus an' gone somewhere else. She always wanted to travel. Talked 'bout Paris an' Venice, but I think she'da been happy just seein' Nashville. I thought for sure she'd be back by the end of that summer. Then when summer came an' went, I thought she'd show up by Christmas, tellin' everybody 'bout what a world traveler she was, how she moved from place to place, pickin' up odd jobs and waitressin' for travel money. That woulda suited Autumn to a T. But she just kept not showin' up and not showin' up, and finally one day, I can't even tell you when, I just knew she was gone. Nobody had a clue what happened to her, and she wasn't never comin' back."

"That sounds...hard." Judith modulated her tone, trying to replicate her sister Constance's easy empathy, but the words were clunky on her tongue. "I'm sure you miss her."

"That's the worst part," Granger said. "I don't. I know I should. Her mama misses her, an' her sister too. But I was just a kid, and she was just the pretty, hot mess of a girl next door. I grew up, moved on. Got a job. She just disappeared one day an' never came back. I should miss her, but I don't."

I don't know how to respond to that, Judith wanted to say. But she knew Constance would say that response was not socially acceptable.

Judith steadied her breath and closed her eyes, sensing for anything radiating from Granger. Emotions, clinging memories –

"You doin' that psychic thing again?"

Judith opened her eyes. "I – I don't have to right now. If you –"

"It just gives me the heebie-jeebies a little bit for you to do it without askin' first, ya know?"

"Of course." Judith moved toward the door. "I should go. You – um, seem busy."

Granger, his body deflated, leaned down to his toolbox again. "Lemme know if you have any more questions, psychic lady."

"Judith. Please just call me Judith."

....

"Miss Temple! Judith!"

Judith paused at the door of her ground-floor motel room. Sheriff Morrissey strode across the parking lot toward her, an ice cream cone in his hand.

"Sheriff," she said. "I wasn't expecting to see you here."

"Best ice cream in town's right across the street."

"You make it sound as though there's more than one ice cream shop."

Tim smiled. "I think there are maybe two other ice cream shops in the whole county. But anyway, I saw you getting ready to enter this lovely establishment and thought I'd run over to let you know that the sheriff's department up in Lexington said they'd take a look at the note if we get 'em some other handwriting samples for comparison."

"'We?'"

"Hey, I wanna have this case solved too. You found some new evidence, so I'll run down answers for you as best I can. You talk to Granger today?"

Judith let out a heavy breath that spun into a sigh. "I did."

Watching her and waiting, Tim took another bite of his ice cream, but she didn't elaborate.

A truck drove by on the nearby street, its massive tires noisy on the uneven asphalt. The sheriff licked away a stray drip of melted ice cream as it dribbled down the side of the cone. "You wanna see McFerrin's tourist attraction?" he said.

"Excuse me?"

"The Swingin' Bridge. Best thing about McFerrin, aside from the ice cream."

"I don't –"

"Come on, walk with me." Tim moved back through the parking lot and headed for the town's main road. He looked back at her over his shoulder with a mischievous grin.

Judith eyed the sun that had sunk almost down to the ridges of the nearby hills. "It's almost sunset. It's getting cold."

"It's just down the block. While we walk, you can tell me what Granger said that's got you all wound up."

"Everything is just down the block here. The whole town is only five blocks end-to-end." Judith followed the sheriff, jogging a few steps to catch up. "And I'm not wound up."

"So what'd he say?"

"That he didn't know anything about the note or what happened to her."

"And that surprised you?"

"No. Of course not. He was just very emotional."

"Emotional?" Tim slowed his walk and turned to look directly at her. "Emotional how?"

"He teared up while talking about Autumn and how hard it's been being the primary suspect for twenty years."

"Oh." A faint frown creasing his face, Tim picked up his walking speed again.

"What did you think I meant by *emotional?*" Judith said.

Tim was quiet as they reached the end of the town proper and made their way down an old paved road toward the river. Here, without the traffic of tires and feet, tree roots and weeds crept up through cracks in the concrete, reasserting their claim to the land as though attempting to swallow the evidence of human encroachment into the forest. Judith peered down the shady hill but couldn't see beyond the next bend in the path.

"He just has a reputation, that's all," Tim said, leading the way into the tunnel of hibernating trees. "I've heard he can get nasty sometimes."

"He's been perfectly pleasant whenever I've talked to him. He said he's been questioned and suspected by every sheriff since Autumn disappeared."

"That's because most people think he's guilty. Or at least that he knows more than he says."

"And do you?"

"Do I what?"

"Think he's guilty."

With a noncommittal shrug, Tim nodded. "Call it a gut instinct."

Judith stopped on the overgrown path. "I beg your pardon?"

"Hm?" Tim turned around.

"You questioned the validity of my readings, despite the fact that I had near-perfect accuracy and had to walk you through how to perform a double-blind test, and yet you base your belief in this man's guilt on *gut instinct*? Please, sheriff, explain to me how that is not wildly hypocritical."

Sheriff Morrissey blinked at her, the rustle of twiggy tree branches filling the sudden silence. A smile cracked across his face, and he turned back to the path. "All right, you might have a point there. Come on, the bridge is just down this way."

Judith stood on the path, her hands still on her hips. Then, with the wind sucked from the sails of her fury, she let out a frustrated huff and hurried after him.

She followed Tim around a sudden hairpin turn, and the overgrown path opened onto a gorge. Below them flowed a muddy brown river, spanned by a rope bridge that stretched to a rocky cliff on the other side.

"This is McFerrin's tourist attraction?" Judith said. "The Swinging Bridge?"

"Swingin' Bridge. Adding that final *g* would make it incorrect."

Judith rolled her eyes. "Very picturesque."

Tim gestured her forward. "After you."

"You want me to walk on that?"

"Thought that's why you came."

"I came because you told me to walk with you."

"Come on, you can't leave McFerrin without visiting the Swingin' Bridge."

Judith peered over the cliff, wondering how this hazard to life and limb could sit so nonchalantly on the outskirts of town. "Is it safe?"

"Sure."

The line where politeness ends and boundaries begin was difficult for Judith to navigate, and the unconcealed, almost childlike satisfaction on the sheriff's face as he finished the last remnant of his ice cream cone was distracting. Judith surveyed the rope bridge, stared down toward the distinctly cold-looking water, and glanced again at Tim. Then, stepping past him, she put a tentative foot on the bridge.

"It's plenty sturdy," Tim said.

Holding tight to the cables that served as railings, Judith scooted forward over the gorge.

Judith felt the bridge shift beneath her feet as Tim stepped on behind her.

"The middle's the best spot," he said.

"For the view?" Judith made the mistake of glancing down, and through the cracks between the wooden boards of the walkway she glimpsed the brown water moving far beneath her feet.

She yanked her gaze back up to the far side of the river and gritted her teeth as she moved forward. There didn't seem to be much of a view to speak of, even as she neared the middle of the bridge. When spring hit full swing, with the now-dormant buds bright green and awake and fragrant, then perhaps the muddy river view would be worth the trek down here, but now, with Kentucky still in the last clutches of winter, she could see nothing spectacular about McFerrin's lone tourist attraction.

Suddenly the world shifted beneath her. Gravity went haywire as the bridge swayed violently to one side, then swung back the other way.

Judith screamed and dropped to a crouch, clutching the cables for dear life.

She was going to die today, her head shattered on rocks lurking just below the surface of the cold brown water. Bleeding out, dragged along by the slow, hungry river –

Behind her came the sound of Tim's laughter. "You okay there?"

The bridge swung again, higher.

Judith turned her head a fraction of an inch over her shoulder. "You're going to kill us!"

A grin on his face, Tim had a hand on each cable, rocking the bridge back and forth like a playground swing. "I told you it's called the Swingin' Bridge. What'd you think it was for?"

"Would you stop that?" Judith shrieked.

After a few more stomach-dropping swings, the bridge's momentum slowed. "Nobody's ever died on here, you know," Tim said. "Every now and then a teenage boy falls off trying to impress a girl, but nobody's ever wound up with more than a few bumps and bruises."

Still crouching, Judith tried to find a way to turn around without letting go of the rope.

Tim stepped toward her with his hand out.

"Stop moving!" Judith froze, clinging to the cables. "You're making it worse!"

Without standing up, Judith began inching back toward the path.

"Walking will get you back faster," Tim said.

"I want to keep my center of gravity low."

"I won't swing it anymore, I promise."

Judith hesitated, then slowly raised herself to a standing position. Still holding tight to the cable, she slid forward while Tim walked backward just in front of her, a poorly-concealed smile on his face.

"Would you stop clomping your feet?" Judith said. "You're making it move again."

"Nothing's gonna break. Except maybe the wooden bits."

Judith's eyes widened as she tested the next board with her foot.

"They're fine, they're fine," Tim said. "See, I'm walking on them right now."

"You mean you're stomping on them."

Tim laughed. "If they can hold me, they'll hold you."

Judith crept the last few feet to the end of the bridge, then darted back onto firm ground. "Don't you dare make some comment about how I should have seen that coming."

"I don't think you need to be a psychic to figure out the purpose of a tourist attraction called the Swingin' Bridge."

"You could've gotten us killed," Judith muttered as she strode back up the path toward town, followed by Tim and his muffled chuckles.

Incensed, Judith whirled back around. "Did you know that, according to Autumn's file, not a single sheriff in the past twenty years has seriously investigated Rock Mitchell in Autumn's disappearance?"

Tim stopped, his smile fading. "How are you defining 'seriously investigated?'"

"Anything beyond writing down his vague alibi for the time of her disappearance, when he claimed he was at home watching TV on the couch and sleeping. As far as I can see, no one has looked into him any further than that."

Tim's hands made their way to his pockets, weariness seeping into his body. "I'm willing to bet the sheriffs who came right after him were hesitant to interrogate one of their own. It's no excuse, just an explanation. And with drugs the way they are around here, I can personally say that a cold case with no leads won't be forefront on any sheriff's mind. I can go with you to talk to Rock, if you like. He might respond better to me."

A sudden tingling like a shower of ice picks rolled down Judith's body. "What did you say?"

"He might respond better to me. You know, a guy. A sheriff. He's kinda old-fashioned, from what I hear."

"You said 'the sheriffs who came right after him.'"

Tim frowned. "I thought you read Autumn's file."

Judith's face grew hot. "I did. But I could have – maybe I missed –" She trailed off.

She'd done it again. Missed something important, something obvious. She could work out problems in her head with the most minute detail, but with the real flesh-and-blood world in front of her, the things which were obvious to everyone else flew by her unseen. Her hands clenched, Judith fought against the rising tide of anger, embarrassment, and frustration within her, threatening to boil over.

"The year Autumn went missing," Tim said, his quiet voice seeming to echo in the claustrophobic tunnel of sleeping trees, "the county sheriff was Rock Mitchell."

VI

THE POEM

*M*ist leeches through the mountains like a living thing, pouring down undulating hills and shrouding the wet-leafed ground, darkened by the clustered trees.

Soft, hungry dirt opens its black mouth, flecked white with blind, clammy, wriggling creatures.

Down, down, far down into the press of the earth.

The open maw closes, and the soil piles, heavy and musty and thick.

Claustrophobic and suffocating, pushing down, down, to the ancient, long-dead leaves heated and hardened beneath the surface of the earth.

Water and soil and coal, deep and dark and heavy.

The last clinging breath pressing out, the blackness crushing down –

The last clinging breath pressed out.

...

Judith sat up in bed, gasping for air. Cold sweat covered her skin, soaking her tangled sheets.

Frantically kicking off her blankets, Judith fought to breathe through the crushing weight on her chest.

In through her nose, out through her mouth – she sucked in air, struggling to regulate her ragged breaths, and the pressure on her lungs slowly dissipated. With shaking hands, she reached to her bedside table and grasped her notebook.

She wrote the date, her usually neat handwriting an untidy, wobbling scrawl. Then she stared at the white page, with its straight black lines waiting to record her data. Clean and sanitized, input and output, data and analysis.

Judith laid the notebook down on the blanket, beside the motley motel comforter that she left folded at the foot of her bed. Slipping out of the sweat-soaked sheets, she moved to the window, where the first gray hint of morning budded over the mountains.

As she watched, the beginning tendrils of sunlight crept over the soft, rolling summits, and her breathing slowed, her heartbeat returning to a steady rhythm. Judith was not easily moved by beauty. A dazzling sunset or a lush, sprawling valley overlook she could acknowledge without the urge to take a second glance. But, as the last frigid clutches of her nightmare receded, something about the dark trees cloaking the mountain and the soft light that rose like a secret over the ridgeline poked beneath her brittle armor.

She watched the sun and the trees and the mountains and the first stirrings of the town outside her window, and a warm tightness built up within her.

Then she shook her head. This was ridiculous. It was a sunrise. The sun rose every morning. And the streets of McFerrin were cracked, the sidewalks were grimy, and the truck that rolled by on the street was rusty and noisy. No need to romanticize a run-down, middle-of-nowhere town.

Judith sniffed and snatched her notebook and pen from the bed.

Dirt
Coal
Buried alive

...

"May I use your copier?" Judith said as she opened the door to the sheriff's office, the bell jingling over her head.

"Hello to you too," Tim said, leaning back in his chair. "You'll have to talk to Cathy about the copier. It's her temperamental child."

Cathy looked at him over her glasses. "You have no reason to be scared of that machine, young man."

"It's the spawn of Satan," Tim said in a stage-whisper.

"It works just fine if you treat it right." Cathy adjusted her glasses and returned her gaze to the stack of paperwork in front of her.

Judith turned to Cathy. "May I use your copier? Please."

"We're not a print shop."

"It's evidence," Judith said. "A handwriting sample from Autumn Hanson. I'd like a copy for myself."

"You got one?" Tim stood from his desk and moved to look over Judith's shoulder.

"Anna May looked through some of Autumn's things and brought it to me. I'm not exactly welcome in the Mitchell house at the moment."

"You don't say," Cathy said under her breath.

"Have you read them yet?" Tim held out his hands for the water-stained manila folder full of yellowed, wrinkled papers that Judith held in her arms.

"I haven't even opened the file," Judith said. "I'm going to get an impression from it before I read it, to prevent bias."

"Oh, that's right." Tim handed the file back. "Why don't you do your thing first, and then I'll make a copy."

Judith chose to ignore the faint skepticism in Tim's voice and took a chair in the corner. She sat with the folder on her lap and closed her eyes.

Blocking out the scrape of Tim's chair on the floor and Cathy's pointed throat-clearing, Judith focused on the papers, whatever their contents might be, and the young woman who wrote them.

Without the strange interference she'd experienced at the Mitchell house, images of Autumn came in a tumble.

Autumn at the small, dingy county high school, dodging out a side door and wandering toward the parking lot.

Autumn, her dark hair tumbling in mussed waves down her back, laughing in a blurry crowd, drawing eyes to her with thoughtless ease.

Autumn in her bedroom, messy with strewn clothes, staring at a sheet of paper, biting her lip, fiddling with the hem of her shirt.

Judith opened her eyes.

A deep undercurrent of *wrongness* flowed through the visions, an unsettled anxiety, a desire for flight and freedom. Claustrophobia, a heavy weight pressing down.

Opening the file, Judith leafed through the faded, watersplotched pages. Scribbled notes to friends. Half-completed school assignments. An unsent letter to an aunt in Michigan.

And a poem.

Judith pulled the paper, torn from a spiralbound notebook, from the folder.

Tiny
Two line surprise
Happy, sad, good, or bad?
Little feet, little hands and heart
Inside

As she read the words, Judith saw Autumn again, biting her lip and worrying the hem of her shirt, pen clutched in her hand.

Judith's eyes flew to Tim, who looked up from his computer.

"What is it?" he said.

Judith stood, crossed the small room, and handed the poem to Tim. Head cocked, he read it. And read it again, his forehead creasing.

"What do you think of this?" Judith said.

"As a poem?" The levity of Tim's words died in the hollow tone of his voice. "From a poetic standpoint, it's pretty basic."

"I'm not interested in it from a poetic standpoint," Judith said. "But, in Autumn's defense, I don't think being county sheriff qualifies you to judge poetic merit."

"Probably not. But, in *my* defense, I've read a fair amount of good poetry."

"You have?" Judith raised her eyebrows.

"Guess you don't quite have me figured out yet, Miss Temple," Tim said. Then his smile faded. Slowly, he set the paper down on his desk, his face weary. "But if you're thinking what I bet you are, I'd say you're probably right."

Standing, he handed the poem and the rest of the folder to Cathy. "Could you make a copy for Judith, please? We need to get this to Lexington."

....

Sunset Holler Boutique was a desperate island of color struggling against the gray sidewalks and crumbling bricks of Salt Fork. Judith pushed through the door into a swirl of pinks and purples and mustard yellows hanging on racks and draped over headless mannequins. A country music station blared through small mounted speakers.

Anna May stood at the counter stacking a pyramid of t-shirts rolled into soft cylinders, and at the tinkling bell of the opening door, she turned with a bright smile. "Welcome! Lookin' for any –" Her eyes met Judith's, and her smile faltered. "Oh – you, um – everythin' okay?"

Judith held out a copy of Autumn's poem. "Have you seen this before?"

Frowning, Anna May took it. "This from the folder? I didn't read through everythin'. Just checked a few things to make sure they were Autumn's and then brought it over to you. I didn't want Rock and my mom to see and get all upset. Is this a poem?"

Anna May went silent, her eyes flying through the words again. Her wide, friendly face paled to a sickly white.

Inside her shoes, Judith curled and uncurled her toes. She should wait, though questions burned within her. Constance would know a delicate way to ask. She would know how to smooth over the thorny sadness, how to soften the hard words. But those were not Judith's strengths.

Judith cleared her throat. "Was Autumn pregnant?"

Anna May heaved a stifled sob, and Judith balled her hands into fists, stabbing her palms with her fingernails. Not this again. Why did everyone in this godforsaken town have to cry?

Suddenly, a chill crept up Judith's skin, and the hair stiffened on her arms. Judith raised her eyes, and the cold turned to ice picks that rolled down her spine, freezing her in place.

Behind Anna May, in a back corner of the shop, was Autumn, her dark hair slick and scraggly, her cheeks pale and dirty. Her stomach glistened with blood.

Judith forced herself to breathe past the crushing weight on her lungs.

"I had no idea," Anna May whispered through tears.

Judith watched the unmoving apparition and her dead-eyed stare.

"She never told me." Anna May shoved the paper back at Judith. "Why didn't she tell me?"

The paper fluttered toward the floor, and Judith snatched it. When her eyes darted back toward the back of the shop, Autumn was gone.

Judith took a trembling breath to steady her voice. "I don't think she had enough time."

...

In a haze, Judith drove to Sloan's Service Station at the very edge of town, the first building to welcome eastbound drivers out of the woods and into Salt Fork.

If Anna May hadn't known about a pregnancy, then maybe someone else had.

In the old convenience store built of dirty white siding and pockmarked concrete, Melissa stood behind the counter, surrounded by magazines, candy bars, and cigarettes.

She turned her face, paler than it had been the previous day, to the door as Judith entered. "You leavin' town or just need gas?"

"I came to talk to you." Scooting past teetering racks of junk food and knick-knacks, Judith made her way to the counter. Even without focusing her awareness, she sensed Melissa's secret, billowing from her in waves of excitement and anxiety.

Perhaps, twenty years ago, Autumn had been pregnant. But today Melissa definitely was. And Judith was not going to break Constance's rule by mentioning it before Melissa said something. She'd already learned that lesson.

Judith stifled a sigh. She hated secrets. They were nasty, festering wounds rotting below the surface of ordinary people. And yet Judith's abilities made her privy to everyone's secrets. "I think Autumn may have learned some important news shortly before her death."

With her fingernail, Melissa picked at a stack of lottery tickets. "Yeah?"

"The kind of news someone might share with a friend."

"Autumn shared personal stuff when she felt like it, but she didn't always feel like it."

Judith sniffed in frustration. So much for beating around the bush. "Was Autumn pregnant shortly before she died?"

Melissa's shoulders stiffened. "I don't know what would make you think that."

"She wrote about it."

"Well, if she wrote about it, why're you askin' me?"

"I'm trying to corroborate it," Judith said. "Do you know if she was pregnant?"

Melissa's lips tightened, and her gaze shifted around the empty store. She narrowed her eyes at Judith as though deliberating. "She never told me nothin' about it one way or the other. But a while before she disappeared, we were hangin' out here –"

"Does this store belong to your family?" Judith said, suddenly remembering Melissa's last name.

"It's my daddy's gas station, yeah. Only one in Salt Fork. But anyway, me and Autumn, we were hangin' out here, and I saw her swipe a pregnancy test, one of those real cheap ones. Never saw what she did with it, and she never talked to me about it. I just remember seein' her slip it into her pocket, thinkin' nobody saw her."

"Who would she have told about a pregnancy?"

"Probably nobody. She could be real secretive about stuff. Wouldn't talk to Rock or her mama for sure, and she didn't like to get Anna May caught up in her messes."

"What do you think she would've done if she had been pregnant?"

Melissa opened and slammed the cash register without touching the money inside, then opened and slammed it again. "Run off to Virginia to get it taken care of, probably."

A dark, angry heat emanated from Melissa like a force field, and Judith instinctively shrunk back.

She watched in silence as Melissa snatched a wet rag and began to scour the mottled vinyl countertop.

"You and Autumn were friends," Judith said at last. "Weren't you?"

"We didn't braid each other's hair and talk about boys, if that's what you mean."

"Then what did you do?"

Melissa scrubbed harder at the counter. "Autumn was fun, okay? She was cool, and people thought she was pretty, and she acted like she didn't care what people thought of her. We hung out because Salt Fork's a small town and we didn't have a lot of options. But she was real closed off. Didn't tell me nothin' that was real, except for the same stuff she was willin' to tell everybody else."

"When did you and Granger..." Judith trailed off.

"Get together? 'Bout a year after she disappeared. He was real broke up about Autumn. But we been together ever since." Melissa strode to a glass case along one wall and pulled out a donut. "You want one?"

Judith shook her head. Melissa shrugged and took a tentative bite of a plain glazed donut. As she chewed, her pale face turned a faint shade of green, and with a grimace she set the nibbled donut on the counter.

"But the thing with Autumn was," Melissa said, "it was always about Autumn. Everythin'. She always had to be in the limelight, and if she wasn't, then she'd go wanderin' off somewhere until people started lookin' for her. Pullin' those kinda stunts didn't work for most girls. Certainly didn't work for me – I tried a coupla times, and nobody even noticed I was gone. But she pulled it off. Got everybody's attention, got them thinkin' about her again. Everythin' was always about her. Even Granger. They'd break up, get back together, break up, get back together, break up – but the second he started makin' eyes at anybody else – boom, there she was gettin' him back again."

"Stewart had a crush on her, didn't he?"

"Every boy in Salt Fork did, and half the boys in the rest of the county."

A foul, prickling question slithered into Judith's thoughts, sickening her stomach. She hesitated, but it roiled within her, trying to force its way out. "If Autumn was pregnant...who was – Would Granger have been the father, or is there any chance it –" Judith paused again, grasping for words. "Could the baby possibly have been her stepfather's? Rock's?"

Melissa gasped. "What?"

"It's awful, I know. Just –"

"I mean, I don't think he ever – They fought all the time, but I never woulda suspected that. But anything's possible, I guess. Did you see that in one of your vision things?"

"No." Judith moved toward the door, her face flushed. "No, I'm just trying to think of other angles. Don't spread it around, please, that I asked about that. I'm just trying to be thorough."

Melissa nodded, her eyes glassy, as Judith pushed back through the door.

Judith escaped to her car once again and sped out of the parking lot, back toward Salt Fork's main street.

She needed to think. And she needed to see Rock, to do a reading on him without the interference at the Mitchell house.

Driving through the strip of buildings and tumbledown houses that made up Salt Fork, Judith steadied her breath and tried to organize her thoughts. As soon as she had a few minutes of quiet, she'd have to take some time to write out a list of suspects, motives, and the readings she'd gotten. Granger, Stewart, Melissa, the horde of unidentified people from the party the night of Autumn's disappearance, and Rock – all of them were suspicious. And yet it was the angry, door-slamming former sheriff, who nobody had been brave or motivated enough to investigate until now, who loomed in Judith's mind. If she could just see him outside of that strange house, if she could just do a reading on him, what kind of turmoil and darkness would she find?

Judith's fingertips began to tingle. Her skin went suddenly cold, colder than the chilly air, and she turned her gaze, drawn as if by gravity, to a narrow gap between two run-down buildings.

There in the shadows stood Autumn, with her dark, tangled hair and her piercing, dead-eyed stare and her seeping, bloody wound.

Judith's stomach roiled, her hands clenching the steering wheel.

"I'm trying," she whispered. "I'm trying, Autumn."

The apparition's eyes followed Judith's as the car moved past.

Judith's car gave a bone-jolting bounce as it hit a deep pothole, and a sudden movement on the street caught her eye. Just outside Fix 'Em Roy's repair shop, Granger leaned against a dark red pickup truck. A cigarette in one hand, he smiled and waved at her.

Judith glanced back into the alley on the other side, but Autumn was gone. The tingling in her fingers lingered, the prickling of pins and needles.

Raising one hand in a quick greeting, Judith pressed on the gas, speeding away from Granger and his casual grin, away from Autumn and the serrated ferocity of her stare, away from the quiet town with a black, twisted secret at its center.

If her online sleuthing from this morning was correct, it was nearly time for Rock's shift as a security guard at the coal mine to end.

Judith drove out of Salt Fork and into the woods, winding through the dark curves of the hills and the thick trees, their first tentative buds just starting to peek out into the brisk air. Following the road up into the mountains, she drove toward the Pine Gap Coal Company and Rock Mitchell.

VII

THE INTERROGATION

The dagger-sharp tips of the mountain pine trees swallowed the last shimmer of daylight, leaving deep folds of darkness in the valley. Harsh, buzzing streetlights flickered to life, illuminating the Pine Gap Coal Company's parking lot in puddles of yellow as Judith sat in her car and watched Rock Mitchell step out of the small, squat security building.

He said goodbye to someone inside, and his low, craggy voice was casual and friendly, butting up like an ill-fitting puzzle piece against Judith's memory of his angry grumblings. Hands in his pockets, he meandered toward the parking lot and sat heavily on a rusty bench, staring out and upward at the mountain and the final orange crescent of light.

Judith closed her eyes.

It was easy now, disconcertingly easy, without the strange static around the Mitchell house. Images and sensations flowed into Judith's mind with the smooth press of a rising tide.

Regret rolled off Rock Mitchell, an undertow of dark, boiling shame and jagged stones.

Cindy at the sink, her back to him, her shoulders sagging with long-carried grief.

Anna May, her face young and smooth, her cheeks plump as ripe peaches, her eyes red with tears, her skin blotched with futile fury.

Cindy, fading to gray, a leaf shriveled to ash in a dying campfire.

Judith pushed further, searching, reaching for Autumn, who hovered like a specter at the edge of Rock's memories.

The incoherent clamor of raised voices, fists banged on tables. Slammed doors, boxes of clothes and books and childhood mementos shoved onto the front porch like a cleansing.

Autumn. Judith strained toward the visions as they flickered and dimmed. *Where are you? What did he do?*

A sharp rap, loud and jarring, on the hood of the car startled Judith from the vision, and she opened her eyes.

Rock Mitchell stood in front of her car, his security uniform rumpled and tight around the abdomen, his face stiff and hard as the gray cliff behind him. "What d'you think you're doin' here?"

Judith clutched the steering wheel, her fingers itching to reach down and put the car in reverse, to escape back onto the road. Peeking around Rock, she glimpsed a trickle of dusty, grime-faced miners stomping out of the cavernous mine entrance as their shift ended. If he tried to get violent, at least there would be witnesses.

Judith rolled down her window a few inches. "I wanted to talk to you."

"I don't want nothin' to do with you, lady. You ain't welcome at my home, and you ain't welcome at my place o' business. Now, you get outta here 'fore I call the sheriff on ya."

"Actually, the sheriff offered to come with me to talk to you," Judith said. "In retrospect, I probably should have taken him up on it."

"What you tryin'a say?"

"He was under the impression that, because he is a sheriff and a man, you might be more willing to talk to him."

"It ain't got nothin' to do with you bein' a female." Rock stepped closer to the cracked window. "I don't wanna talk to you 'cause you're a vulture hangin' around, leechin' money outta my family."

"Anna May is the one paying me, and, as far as I'm aware, she's not your daughter."

The only part of Rock that moved were his hands, clenching into fists. "You get outta here," he hissed, "and don't you come back."

Rock turned away, stalking back toward the metal bench.

Frustration surged through her, and Judith yanked the keys from the ignition and opened her door. "I have questions for you."

Rock kept walking, hands shoved into his pockets.

Judith closed her car door, which beeped as it locked. "Why did you wait a month before you labeled Autumn a missing person?"

Walking faster, Rock did not sit on the bench, but strode around it, keeping it between them like a shield, his back to her. His bulky shoulders rose and fell with heavy breaths.

Judith followed him, standing on the opposite side of the bench. "Why did you give the case four weeks to go cold before you even tried to look into your own stepdaughter's disappearance?"

Rock spun around to face her and clutched the back of the bench with white-knuckled hands. "You don't know nothin' 'bout her." His constricted voice stabbed into the air, too loud in the chill, quiet evening air. "Get back in your fancy car and crawl back to whatever city you came from."

"First of all," Judith said, "it's not a fancy car. It's lightly used. Buying brand new cars is a waste of money. And secondly, I do know that Autumn periodically disappeared for a few days while she couch-surfed. And I also know that you kicked her out of the house on multiple occasions. But there's a big difference between someone with Autumn's history going missing for a few days, and going missing for a month without a word. So what took you so long?"

"I ain't talkin' to you. If you're accusin' me of somethin', you go get your sheriff and have him come say it to my face."

"Everythin' okay?" said a voice.

Startled, Judith turned her eyes away from Rock to the handful of dirt-covered men in dusty coveralls standing nearby, their eyes shifting between the scene before them and their cars in the parking lot.

"Your ride comin' soon, Rock?" one of them said.

Judith crossed her arms and turned back to Rock. "I could do that. I could go get the sheriff. Would you talk to him? Would you tell him why you didn't investigate until it was too late?" A strange, small buzzing pushed at the edge of Judith's awareness, and her fingertips went numb.

"Get outta here, lady." Rock's hands tightened on the back of the bench.

"Were you buying time?" Judith said, pushing past the distracting, fuzzy clamor in her mind. "Were you destroying evidence?"

"I said get outta here."

"Where did you hide her body, Rock?"

"You shut your mouth!" Suddenly Rock was around the bench, and one of the miners, his thick neck caked with dust and streaked with sweat, was between them, arms out like a wall.

Judith fell back a step, delayed adrenaline flooding her body at the fury in Rock's voice and the raging speed in his steps. Beside the growing audience of miners and bear-shouldered Rock, she was small, a lone woman with nothing but her car keys as a weapon.

The buzzing in Judith's mind grew, a noisy static pressing into her thoughts. Judith fought back against it, focusing her attention on Rock as, behind her back, she squeezed her key fob and unlocked her car. "You killed Autumn, didn't you?"

A strangled, gasping sound came from behind Judith, and the static rose to a fever pitch, stabbing at her mind.

She whirled around, and behind her stood Cindy, white-faced and wide-eyed. Clutching her purse to her chest, Cindy backed up, her legs shaking as she rasped with ragged breaths.

Judith gaped at Cindy and her deathly pale face.

The static, the interference, the buzzing that disrupted Judith's visions –

It wasn't the house. It wasn't the house at all.

A heavy arm shoved Judith out of the way, and she stumbled sideways as Rock barreled toward Cindy.

"Don't touch me!" Cindy shrieked, collapsing to the weed-infested sidewalk, her back against a light post. She breathed in sharp, jagged gasps, her hand at her chest, and a sob wracked her body. "What did you do?"

"Honey –" Rock reached out toward Cindy but stopped as she wailed and shrank away from him.

Heat and the thick scent of burnt earth radiated from behind Judith, and over her shoulder came the menacing rumble of a voice. "Get out."

Judith turned, backing away as one of the miners advanced on her, pointing at her car.

"Get outta here, and don't come back."

Judith's legs shook as she stumbled to her car and fumbled with the door handle. Cindy's panicked sobs grew louder, and Rock's sandpaper voice hollered for an ambulance.

Looking back once more, Judith locked eyes with the largest of the miners, his body squared with hers and his face hard as stone. She scrambled into her car, threw it into drive, and sped out of the parking lot, back onto the dark country road.

Heart pounding, Judith suddenly screeched to a halt as she realized that she couldn't see anything but the dim gray outline of the trees and the hills. She turned on her car headlights, and the tangled forest lit up in cones of yellowed light. She peeled away again on the deserted road, the deafening static in her mind fading as she put distance between herself and Cindy.

Cindy –

Who was she?

What was she?

Had Judith just killed her, her heart giving out at the realization that she was married to her daughter's murderer?

Judith's foot seemed unable to accelerate or slow down smoothly as she stomped on the gas and then the brake, making her stomach churn around the tight turns of the mountain road. Her hands trembled, her face hot and flushed as she wound her way toward Salt Fork.

Food. She needed food and rest, and she'd be fine. She just needed to make it back to McFerrin and her motel room. Then she'd eat dinner, write down her visions, and figure out what on earth was going on with Cindy. She'd figure out all of it. She just needed quiet.

Judith bit her lip. She should have taken Tim with her. What had she been thinking? She wasn't an officer of the law. She was just a software engineer who sometimes saw things she couldn't explain.

Judith slowed to the speed limit as she entered Salt Fork, dormant and still as a ghost town in the evening twilight. She drove past Fix 'Em Roy's car repair shop, past Anna May's Sunset Holler Boutique.

The jittering in her hands eased, and her breathing calmed, though her thoughts roiled within her. She'd categorize her visions, input them into her spreadsheet - that's what she'd do. Then she'd reason her way through it all. Everything would be fine. Everything would be clear.

Judith's fingers tingled and went numb.

Sloan's Service Station loomed ahead of her, its dirty white façade glowing faintly in the first hint of moonlight. A dark red pickup truck was parked in front of it.

A chill leeched into Judith's skin, and she let out a weary sigh, her shoulders sagging. Knowing what she would see, she looked up, and there, by the side of the road, was Autumn, dead-eyed and bloody, her dark hair lank and dirty.

"What?" Judith whispered, a seething fury in her voice. "What do you want from me?"

Slamming on the brakes, Judith pulled the car to the side of the road and parked. "Is this what you want?" Heaving in tight, angry breaths, she stared directly back at Autumn and her ravaged body that shimmered in the car's headlights. "If you want to tell me something, then just tell me."

Judith closed her eyes and tried to loosen the knot in her body, tried to quiet the riotous waves of her thoughts and listen.

It came in a flutter at first, a flickering image.

Fire, orange flames licking at the peeling blue paint of a small house.

The vision grew, the colors brightening, the sound sharpening. A little freckled boy with eyes the deep pine green of the mountains, a woman with a swelling secret within her, sleeping as smoke crept under the door.

A man, his face a strange, familiar echo – a horrible, off-kilter brokenness in his eyes. Something tilted, not quite right.

Then the image swirled and shifted, and sound dug into Judith's ears as she saw through someone else's eyes.

The night sky, stars poking through the trees, pine needles and dirt slamming hard against her back.

The scrape of metal, the glint of moonlight on a deadly sharp edge –

Screams, disturbing nothing but the trees and the squirrels that dodged back into their homes –

Blood, too much blood, and ragged breaths and dirt catching under her fingernails and a grave-dark hole in the earth.

And eyes, pine green and off-kilter, face swimming in and out of view, until suddenly she was above him, watching his lean body, his oil-covered hands, yank the blood-slick knife out of her.

Judith's eyes flew open. Gasping, she grasped her stomach.

Still intact. No blood. No needles in her hair, no dirt crusted under her fingernails.

Cold sweat beaded over Judith's forehead and dripped down her neck.

It couldn't be. How could she have missed it? She should have known, should have seen –

There was movement outside her car, and Judith's gaze darted toward it with a start.

Autumn was gone, the night dark and still. But, just ahead of Judith, the lights of Sloan's Service Station were bright as the door opened. Granger strode out, his arm slung over Melissa's shoulder, a cigarette between his fingers.

He paused, his eyes lingering on Judith's car in the dimness, and he threw up his hand in greeting.

A shiver cascaded down Judith's spine, and her breath caught in her throat.

She put the car into drive once more and sped toward McFerrin. Her hands were ice cold, her body coiled tight as a mouse trap.

It couldn't be.

But her mind flew back to Autumn, to her dead-eyed stare, to her bloodied body, to her last moments, when a boy with pine green eyes knelt over her, holding a knife in his hands, his fingernails dirty with engine oil –

The last thing Autumn saw that night, deep in the lonely, claustrophobic woods, was Granger Combs.

VIII

THE TURNING

Judith's shoulders were tight, her fists clenched, and her crusty eyes strained with lack of sleep when she barreled through the door of the sheriff's office the next morning.

Tim Morrissey sat behind his desk, an open file in front of him and the warm, cozy scent of fresh coffee filling the small office. "This is getting to be a habit of yours," he said, "showing up here first thing in the morning to demand stuff."

He looked up with the hint of a smile, but it dropped away at the sight of Judith's face. "What's wrong? Something happen?"

Judith winced. She hated when people could read her so easily, when her body language betrayed her. Another piece of her armor gone, lost to this language that everyone else seemed to speak fluently but which she had to study and analyze just to grasp at its meaning.

Judith eased herself into the chair on the opposite side of Tim's desk. "I learned something."

"Is this about Rock Mitchell? Or Cindy?"

Judith sucked in a small breath of air, a flush of heat coursing through her and settling in a guilty ball in her stomach. She hadn't even thought about Rock, about Cindy wailing beneath the fluorescent lights of a parking lot. Not since last night when she'd peeled off the road, daring Autumn, with her bloody, dirt-smeared body and her dead-eyed stare, to make everything clear. "You heard about that?"

"It's a small county. Just like the sheriff's office and motel, the only ambulance is in McFerrin."

"So they did call an ambulance," Judith said, biting her lip and stabbing her palm with her fingernails. It helped, sometimes, when the world was tilted, spinning slowly and relentlessly out of control, to have a sharp point of pain, a distraction under her control. "Is she –?"

"I haven't heard."

Judith shifted in her seat. "It's not about Cindy. Or Rock."

Silent and inscrutable, Tim watched her, waiting.

The words Judith had rehearsed in the small, dark hours of the morning in her motel room, and again as she sat in her car in the parking lot, dropped from her mind like sidewalk chalk sprayed by a gush of water. She glanced around the quiet office. "Where's Cathy?"

Tim's faint smile returned. "Did you forget what day it is?"

"It's Saturday."

"Yeah."

"Oh." Judith stared at her hands, at the nails she'd spent years training herself not to chew, now gnawed down to the nubs. "I forgot."

"You forgot?"

"I forgot that most people don't come to work on Saturday," Judith said. Then, before she could second guess or over-analyze the words, she forced them out. "I saw Granger Combs. In a vision. I saw him pull the knife out of Autumn the night she died."

Tim's eyes dropped to the file on his desk, and gravity seemed to tug a little harder on him as he exhaled a faint sigh, a grim chuckle. "Wouldn't you know."

Judith waited, but Tim did not elaborate.

Lack of sleep and the unrelenting knot in her stomach poked at her, prickling her skin. "Please explain. I'm not in the mood and have not had enough sleep to interpret cryptic remarks."

"You want some coffee?" Tim pushed back his chair and strode to a small coffee maker and mini-fridge sitting on a rickety table in the corner.

"I suppose so. Thank you." Judith sank back against the stiff wooden back of the chair.

While Tim pulled two mugs out of a cabinet and poured the coffee, Judith's thoughts derailed from the case, away from Granger and Rock and the eerie interference that seemed to be emanating from Cindy in a way Judith couldn't explain, to the muddled niceties of coffee. She'd already said *thank you*; would she have to thank Tim again when he handed her the coffee? Would two *thank you*'s be excessive?

How did the vast majority of people seem to stride through the act of thanking someone for coffee without any visible signs of distress? Why couldn't she just thank someone for coffee like a normal person? Like Constance.

Dragging her thoughts away from questions to which she had no answer, Judith fixed her eyes on Tim. "Are you going to explain yourself?" she said.

"I need some coffee first." Tim returned with two sloshing mugs in his hands and a container of creamer balanced precariously under his chin.

Handing Judith a mug, brown drips slipping down its sides, he sat, sipped his coffee, and took a breath. "I came in this morning to read up more on Granger. I dug through some old files, found everything I could on him –"

"Why?"

"Gut instinct. It was like an itch I had to scratch, just couldn't rest until I found out more about him. I think he's bad news."

"You're saying you just happen to be here on a Saturday morning, digging through old files about Granger Combs at the same time that I come to talk to you about him? But your 'gut instinct' is somehow irreproachable, whereas what I do is questionable at best?"

Far from getting any kind of rise out of Tim, he only chuckled. "Hey, I've been impressed by your accuracy so far. But I don't charge people money for my gut instinct."

"Yes, you do. You're doing it right now. But for you, the taxpayers are paying the bills."

"It's a tiny fraction of my job, at most. The vast majority of my job these days is paperwork." He gestured toward his desk and clunky computer. Then he glanced down at the file again, and his smile faded. "I think maybe you oughta take a look at this. But – just to warn you – it's not good."

"There was a fire."

Tim's eyes, suddenly flinty, sprang to her face.

"His father set it," Judith said. "The house was blue. Granger survived, but his mother didn't."

Tim sat back in his chair and passed a hand over his mouth.

"And –" Judith hesitated, the words brutal and ugly on her tongue. "His mother was pregnant."

Tim let out a breath. "I didn't know that. I'll have to check the death certificate."

"She was."

"I'm not saying I don't believe you. But I still have to check." Tim passed the file to Judith. "You wanna take a look?"

Without even summoning the energy to suggest that she do a psychic reading of the file, Judith took it and flipped it open.

"I can give you the summary," Tim said, leaning back in his seat, nursing his coffee. "Dad went to prison after the fire, got himself killed in a prison fight at some point during the next few years. Granger got passed around to different foster homes. About the time he was in middle school, he found a family that stuck, somewhat. An older couple who took three or four foster kids at a time, mostly for the money from the state. He stayed with them until he graduated high school and moved out. Now he fixes cars and sells Oxy. And, apparently, commits murder."

The knot in Judith's stomach began to pulsate, heat roiling like the steam of a teapot, straining for release. "This is exactly why people accuse law enforcement of tunnel vision."

Tim blinked. "What?"

"He had a traumatic childhood, and when you need a suspect, that's all you see. You don't think to look at other angles."

"You said you had some vision where you saw Granger pulling a knife out of Autumn."

"Pulling a knife out," Judith said. "I don't know who put it in."

Tim stared at her, his coffee forgotten. "Are you saying that you claim to have seen a vision of Granger Combs pulling a knife out of Autumn, and you still think he's innocent?"

"My visions give fragments of the truth, often colored by other people's perceptions, or even my own. They rarely tell the full story. But if I'm looking for something specific during my readings, I almost always find it if it's there. When I did a psychic reading on Granger, I didn't get a single hint of Autumn's murder."

"A psychic reading? Have you *met* the guy? He's nobody's fool. He can be friendly when he wants to be – and some people think he's decent-looking, I guess – but he's not someone you should trust."

"It seems to me that you're not being very objective about Granger Combs as a suspect," Judith said. "What does his appearance have to do with anything?"

Tim cleared his throat. "Nothing. But if you think Granger supposedly pulled a knife out of a dying woman and then concealed that fact for twenty years, he's at least guilty of obstruction of justice."

"Yes, but obstruction of justice isn't murder."

"You're just going to ignore the fact that he's a convicted felon who sells drugs to addicts all up and down this county?"

"Unless that fact is relevant to this case," Judith said, her jaw tight, "then yes, I am."

Tim pushed back his chair and stood, striding to the small window with its cheap white vinyl blinds. He pulled off his hat and ran an agitated hand through his hair. Then, staring out the window, a ruminative frown passed like a cloud over his face.

Judith squeezed her hands together in her lap. In the diner, back when she'd done her reading of Granger, she hadn't felt any of the leeching darkness that murder would leave in a person's psyche. He was a talkative, bacon-burger-eating open book. There had been nothing at all like murder in him. What *had* she seen in her reading of Granger? She couldn't quite recall.

Turning, Tim fixed a weighty, thoughtful gaze on Judith. "At eighteen, if *I* had come upon my dying girlfriend, I would've tried to get help. I would've called the sheriff as soon as I could. And I would've left the knife in, because any idiot with the slightest knowledge of wounds would know that pulling it out could kill her." He took a long, deep breath and pulled his hat back onto his head, covering up his now-messy hair. An unexpected twinge strangely similar to disappointment panged somewhere in the vicinity of Judith's chest. "But a kid with Granger's history – you may be right. His first instinct might have been to run."

Judith cocked her head, a sudden nagging realization poking into her memories.

"What is it?" Tim said.

There he was again, interpreting her facial expressions and making suppositions about her state of mind. It was quite annoying. But, pushing aside her irritation at her own transparency, Judith reached into her purse and pulled out her notebook. She flipped through it, scanning the visions she'd recorded over the past week.

The knot in Judith's stomach tightened, and her lethargic mind began to buzz with the certainty that she was missing a crucial piece of a solvable puzzle. She looked up at Tim.

"I just remembered something," she said. "I never completed a reading on Granger."

···

The rhythmic squeak of a twisting wrench guided Judith through Fix 'Em Roy's garage to where Granger bent over the open hood of a dented pickup truck.

At the sound of her footstep, he glanced over his shoulder. "Psychic lady! You're back."

"It's *Judith*," she said. "I'd like to do another reading on you. If you have a minute."

Granger straightened and turned around, leaning against the hood of the car. Engine oil spattered his coveralls and the sleeves of the shirt that poked out over his arms, but his body moved with the casual, athletic grace of a person unafraid to take up space.

A flutter of envy flitted through Judith. Never in her life had she taken up space with such unabashed ease. Her presence was an intrusion, an awkward ornament hung crookedly in a space not designed for her.

"Thought you already did your readin' thing," Granger said.

"I never completed it. You were quite talkative that morning, and it disrupted my process."

Granger chuckled. "Sorry 'bout that. Me and my mouth. Can't do nothin' 'bout it. Lotsa people've tried over the years."

Granger, leaning over Autumn in her dying moments, pulling a knife from her bleeding stomach – Judith quashed the memory, shoving it down. There must be some reason, some other explanation. Not Granger, not this man in front of her, lackadaisical and grinning and covered in engine oil. "If you could go about your work, or whatever would help you to stay distracted and quiet, I'll just do my reading and be on my way."

"Why you wanna do that now? Thought you figured out Rock Mitchell was the guy?"

"Who told you that?"

"It's a small town. News travels real quick out here, 'specially when there's an ambulance involved."

Judith took a breath, trying to loosen the lingering tightness in her chest. "I do suspect Rock Mitchell. I don't think he has been sufficiently investigated by law enforcement. But I saw something, something involving you, and I want to finish my reading so that I can know what really happened."

"What d'you mean you saw something?"

Shifting her weight between her feet, Judith pressed her fingernails harder into her palm. That had been incredibly stupid. Why had she said that? And why couldn't she come up with an easy lie to cover it up? Words floundered on her tongue, until, in a gush, she pushed out the bare truth. "I know you were with Autumn when she died."

Granger didn't blink, but his body went taut as a wire.

Judith's fingertips turned numb, and she couldn't uncurl her hands from the tight fists she'd made. She lowered her voice to disguise its shaking. "I want to hear your side of the story. Did you find her and then cover up her death? Tell me what happened."

"What d'you mean you *know* I was with her?" Granger's expression didn't move, his voice flat. "What – you *saw* me or somethin'? In one of your visions or whatever you call 'em?"

"Yes. I saw you when – Well, never mind. You tell me what you remember. If I know the truth, then I can start to get to the bottom of what really happened to Autumn that night."

Granger's shoulders crumpled, and a sheen rose in his eyes.

Judith bit her lip. Not tears again.

"Look, I –" Granger faltered, his voice breaking. "I don't remember much about that night, really. We were doin' some hard stuff, stuff we shouldn'ta been doin', and it messed with my head. I get these flashes sometimes, of Autumn –" Granger pinched the bridge of his nose and squeezed his eyes shut.

Judith stared at her shoes, suddenly acutely aware that she had nothing to do with her ungainly hands and that inside her shoe one of her socks had folded itself under her pinky toe.

Granger took a shaky breath. "But I always thought it was a bad dream, like maybe I was just imagining – You didn't tell the sheriff, did you? He'll be on me just like the others, and I don't remember nothin'. I won't be no help in clearin' my name. What did you see, in your vision thing?"

"Why don't you let me do a reading," Judith said, trying to modulate her voice. Constance could smooth her tone, lower her volume, in a way that calmed a room and brought high emotions back into check. With the right words, the right tone, surely Judith could do it too. "Maybe I can fill in those gaps in your memory. Your subconscious might have retained more of those memories than your conscious mind."

"Look, you just came in here while I'm supposed to be workin' and told me you think I saw my girlfriend die in the woods twenty years ago. I ain't in no state of mind for no psychic reading."

"I'm just trying to piece together this puzzle. With a little more information, I could help clear your name, and then no one could accuse you of this crime again."

Granger scoffed. "You been in this town a week now, and you still think I could live here without people whisperin' behind my back? That ain't how Salt Fork works."

"If someone else is arrested, tried in a court of law, and found guilty, why would anyone still suspect you?"

With a bitter chuckle, Granger shook his head. "I dunno if you're a true believer in them lawyers and judges, or just don't know nothin' 'bout the real world, but Salt Fork decided a long time ago that I'm guilty."

"Just let me do a reading, and –"

"I ain't doin' no readin' right now."

At the vehemence in his voice, Judith drew back.

"Look," he said, the tears popping back into his eyes, "maybe after work. Just not right now. I'm right in the middle of fixin' up this truck, and my brain's all over the place, with you bringin' all this up again. Later. Come by later. But lemme get back to work."

"This is my last full day in Salt Fork, Granger. I'm running very short on time."

"I don't want you pokin' and proddin' around in my brain right now. If havin' you rootin' around in my head ends up givin' me nightmares of Autumn dyin' out in them woods, I don't think I can take it."

"I've never had a client experience nightmares as a direct result of one of my readings. I won't say there's a zero percent chance of it happening, because that would be intellectually dishonest, but I can safely say that it is extremely unlikely."

"Not now." Granger crossed his arms. "Come back later, like I said."

Frustration crept into Judith, tightening her already tense body. "What makes you so resistant to a psychic reading?"

"How many times do I gotta explain myself to you?" Granger turned back to the car and took up the wrench once more. Then, shoulders sagging, he turned around again, and a trickle flowed from one of his eyes, rolling down his cheek as he sniffed and wiped it away with his sleeve. "Later. I ain't in no state to do this now."

Judith's fingertips began to tingle again. She frowned, pressing her lips together. "I'll come back at five."

Judith turned to leave, making her way through the small garage stuffed with rust-spotted cars and dented fenders. An insistent prickling sensation tugged at her, needling her skin, and she steeled herself to catch a glimpse of dead-eyed Autumn lurking in the shadows. But Autumn didn't appear, and the dim corners of the shop were empty aside from old, clunky cars.

Emerging into the chilly light of early spring, Judith stepped aside from the door of the garage and stood with her back against the concrete blocks of the building. She needed to be close, as close as she could without Granger seeing her.

Judith closed her eyes, reaching out, focusing her mind on Granger, emptying it of all else, making space for impressions to wash over her.

For a few moments, she saw nothing, felt nothing except the faint warmth of the sun straining against the cold air. Then, like a wave rushing up a beach, it came.

A flicker, like a stuttering film reel. Faint images, muffled sounds – *flames licking peeling wallpaper, screams, the crash of a door bursting open and the crushing force of smoke-scented arms.*

The relentless wish – that the fire had taken him too. He was meant to die, the poisoned spawn of a hateful man.

Then, the images changed.

Pine needles, soft and silent underfoot. Long, dark hair, shimmering with moonlight.

Within, roiling, overpowering fear, rising with relentless tidal power –

The poisoned spawn of a hateful man – the cycle would end with him.

Moonlight, flashing on metal

Autumn's eyes, widening, panicking

The wet slice of sharp metal piercing flesh –

Again

Again

Again

The poisoned spawn of a hateful man –

"What're you still doin' here?"

Judith opened her eyes, ice cascading through her body.

Granger stood beside her on the sidewalk.

Judith forced the horror from her face – closed her mouth, blinked her eyes, struggled for control – but she knew she was too late.

Granger's eyes flicked down the length of her, over her clenched fists and feet rooted to the ground, and back up, over her face drained of color and eyes no longer seeing innocence in his.

His face didn't move, but it changed. The teary sheen in his eyes was gone, evaporated to a calculated, razor-edged leer, his smile hardening in place. Still as marble, but suddenly tilted, broken, off-kilter – a veil slipping away. "I asked you what you're still doin' here."

Judith, her throat frozen, backed up toward her car, parked along the side of the empty road.

"It ain't real, ya know." Granger stepped toward her, a heavy wrench still clutched in his hand.

Had he always been this big, dwarfing her like a lone tree beside a mountain?

"Your visions, your readings, whatever you call 'em. They ain't real. And ain't no sheriff or judge or jury ever gonna listen to you."

A black SUV rumbled along the road, splitting the silence, and Judith darted to her car, unlocking and clambering in – quickly, while there were witnesses.

Locking the door, she threw it into *drive*, her thudding heartbeat drowning out all other sounds as she peeled away. She accelerated down the street, not knowing whether she was driving into Salt Fork or out of it.

In the rearview mirror, the black SUV had parked on the side of the street, and Granger stood on the sidewalk, arms crossed, eyes following her until she rounded a curve and disappeared among the trees.

Judith's body thrummed with a swirling, congealed jumble of terror and certainty.

Granger – it had been Granger, all along.

Granger, chatty and personable, throwing his arm around Melissa. Granger, teary with regret and shame, lamenting how he didn't mourn Autumn as he should.

Granger, the broken, lonely boy whose own father had tried to kill him.

As the mountains sped by in a rush of brown and the first hints of fresh spring green, Judith's heartbeat began to slow, and her ears caught the buzz of her phone ringing.

Judith pulled onto the shoulder of the country road and snatched her phone with shaking hands. "Hello?"

Anna May's voice was brittle as ice over a puddle. "We need to talk."

"I know who killed Autumn –"

"Yeah, you made sure everybody in town knows what you think. And you don't got no proof for any of it, do you?"

"It wasn't Rock. I was –" Judith's throat clenched. "I was wrong."

"Well, that's great. That fixes everythin'. You got my mama sent to the hospital, you know that?"

"I didn't know Cindy was going to be there."

"Thank the Lord it wasn't a heart attack, or I would've sued you for everythin' you've got."

The unconcealed venom in Anna May's voice was palpable, and Judith's thoughts glitched. She spewed out the first words that came to mind. "I don't think you would have sufficient grounds for a lawsuit."

"It was a panic attack, thanks for askin'. A panic attack *you* caused. She kicked Rock outta the house, and he's sleepin' on his friend's couch. He's a mess. He didn't go to work today, and he ain't never missed a day of work in his life. And my mama hasn't left her bed." Anna May's volume dropped, and dread jolted through Judith – somehow, the quiet was sharper, more violent. "You. You're tearin' my family apart. You get out of Salt Fork today, and don't you ever let me hear from you again."

The phone clicked and went silent.

Judith's hands were chilled, her fingers curling into fists. Her lips were numb with cold, the center of her body radiating heat.

No, she couldn't stop – not now. Not when she knew –

Her hands shook, her vision blurring as she struggled to navigate her phone.

A text message dinged, the name *Timothy Morrissey (Sheriff)* emblazoned across her phone.

Everything okay? it said. *That looked tense.*

With sudden, numb clarity, Judith recognized the black SUV. An unmarked sheriff's vehicle.

Tim hadn't let her come alone after all. But the realization neither surprised nor comforted her as she ignored the text, blinked to clear her vision, and struggled through the contacts of her phone.

Holding the phone to her ear, Judith gasped to steady her breath, but her lungs hitched, squeezing, throttling.

"Hello-ooo!" A voice sang on the other end. "I'm in the middle of cookie baking, so if I – no no, honey, just a little bit of salt, let Mommy do it – so if I scream and the line goes dead, it's probably because there's flour all over the floor. But how *are* you?"

Judith, her eyes burning – why were they burning? – tried to speak, but no sound escaped her tight throat.

Constance's voice lost its sing-songy tone, suddenly serious. "Judith? What's wrong?"

Judith didn't cry. She didn't cry. Other people cried, and she hated it, but she didn't cry.

But her eyes were burning and there was salty water on her face and her chest was heaving, and all of her words were swallowed by the sobs that shook her shoulders.

IX

THE GOODBYE

Deep orange traced the mountain ridge above McFerrin as Tim Morrissey knocked on Judith's motel room door. Her car was still in the motel parking lot, though she was supposed to have been two hours away, back in Lexington by now. But Tim's faint rumbles of misgiving faded when Judith cracked open the door, the chain at the top still locked in place.

Tim held up a bag. "I brought donuts."

"Why?"

"Because everybody likes donuts, and you've had a rough couple of days."

A crease popped between Judith's eyebrows. "There are six donuts in that bag. I'll only eat one, so I hope you weren't planning on eating five."

Tim cocked his head, assessing the bag's contents, and shrugged. "Maybe not in one sitting."

"Do you know how many grams of sugar are in the average glazed donut?"

"Why would I ever want to know the answer to that question?"

"Because eating five donuts in one day would put you well over your recommended daily sugar intake."

"Can I come in?"

Judith hesitated for a moment, then unlocked the chain and opened it for him.

Tim stopped just inside the door. Just by existing inside it, Tim turned every hotel room he ever stayed in into a messy disaster within minutes. But despite the fact that Judith had been living out of this motel room for a week, both of the queen-sized beds were neatly made, and all of her personal belongings, from her suitcase perched on the luggage rack to her bag of dirty laundry tucked into an unobtrusive corner, were as organized as if she'd just unpacked.

But spread over the cramped desk, piled on the floor, and scattered across the unused bed were papers.

"I thought you were planning to go back to Lexington today," Tim said.

"I extended my stay an extra night. I'll drive back in the morning." Chewing on her lip, Judith watched Tim observe the state of the motel room. "I like to have everything in front of me when I'm thinking."

Judith slipped by him to extricate a chair from the maze of papers.

It was then that Tim finally got a good look at her, rather than just her eye peeking through a cracked door.

Her hair was in a ponytail, and her face was bare of makeup. Instead of her crisp, tailored business casual attire, she wore sweatpants and a thick, fluffy sweatshirt. It was strange – seeing her without armor, with her mask slipped away.

Judith set the chair down outside the ring of papers and then sat on the edge of the bed.

Pulling the chair closer as he sat, Tim opened up the bag of donuts. "One of everything the convenience store had. Take your pick."

When Judith had pulled a chocolate cake donut from the bag and he had settled on a Long John, Tim leaned back in his chair. "You look different."

Judith frowned. "I don't know how to respond to that."

"No, it's a good thing," Tim said. "I've just never seen you being comfortable, just hanging out, before."

"I'm not *hanging out*." Judith pointed to the papers on the desk. "Those are copies of all relevant available public records." Her finger moved to the floor. "Those are interview notes." She gestured to the bed. "Those are my personal records of my visions and readings. There's something here, somewhere, that can get me evidence against Granger."

"That's not your job." Tim rested his elbows on his knees. "It's mine. And I'll keep working on it for as long as it takes, which, in a case like this, might be a long time."

"Anna May hired me to figure out what happened to Autumn."

"And you did that. But you're not working for her anymore."

"You're telling me that Granger just gets to walk around town selling drugs and fixing cars indefinitely until you find evidence against him?" Judith said.

"That's how it works."

"But he's guilty."

"I believe you. But if we try to bring a case against him too soon, before it's substantial enough to really nail him, it's not gonna do any good."

Judith took an agitated bite of her donut and lapsed into silence.

Tim looked down at his hands. "Did I ever mention I was in the army?"

"No."

"Well, I was. Right out of high school. Spent some time overseas."

"About which, I assume, you can't go into detail?"

"That's a pretty fair assumption," Tim said, smiling. "Not everybody who was over there with me had good intentions, but I had a CO who was one of the best. And he said that, whatever might happen after, it was our job to leave a place better than we found it."

"Did you?"

That old weariness that dragged at Tim's shoulders, springing up suddenly like gravity trying to pull him into the molten core of the earth. "I thought we did. But it didn't last long."

Judith picked a crumb from the bedspread. "Was this supposed to relate to my situation?"

"It was," Tim said, a chuckle loosening the weight on his shoulders. "I guess I lost track of where I was going with that."

Judith smiled then, a small smile breaking across her impassive face. And suddenly Tim wanted to do whatever it took to make her smile again.

"What did you do when you left the army?" Judith said.

"Studied forestry, believe it or not. I was a park ranger for a good while. But really, I just needed quiet. And lots of wild green land. I'd seen some ugly things overseas, and that's a heavy weight on somebody who's barely more than a kid." Tim leaned back in his chair, shrugging off his somber tone. "Then one day I got the harebrained idea to run for county sheriff, and, for some reason, they elected me."

"You're familiar with the area and have military experience," Judith said. "Presumably that's why they elected you."

"Well, when you put it that way, it sounds almost reasonable."

Judith nodded, and silence slipped over the room once again.

"When I was in middle school," Judith said at last, knitting her fingers together in her lap, "it wasn't a good period in my life – the social dynamics, the cliques. You may have noticed that I'm not the most naturally sociable person."

Tim couldn't help the smile that tugged at his mouth, but he said nothing.

"But the summer before my eighth-grade year," Judith said, "I snuck onto my family's home computer to watch tutorial videos. I learned how to curl my hair, how to apply mascara, eyeliner, eye shadow. And during the fall semester, I found that there was a 66.67% decrease in snide remarks, distasteful pranks, and similar behaviors directed toward me."

She raised her eyes from her tightly woven fingers and looked up at Tim. "If there's anything I know, it's that if certain actions yield a desirable result, then I should keep performing those actions to achieve that same result. So yes, as you said, I look different today." She gestured to the papers stacked around the room. "Because I was concerned about working out how to prove this case, not about trying to convince people to take me seriously."

Tim's face grew hot, and he leaned forward on his elbows again. "I put my foot in my mouth. I'm sorry. What I meant was that it's nice, getting to see you, just you."

"Did I do that right?" Judith said. "You shared a bit of your background, so I shared some of mine?"

At the hint of sarcasm in her voice, Tim looked up with an exaggerated gasp. "Are you - *joking*?"

"It's not a *joke*. It's a question that is somewhat tongue-in-cheek."

"I didn't think you *did* jokes."

"I have a sense of humor. I'm not a robot." Judith's eyes roved again over the papers littering the room. The faint smile faded, the crease between her eyebrows returning. "I was supposed to find her."

"Find Autumn?"

Judith nodded.

"Judith," Tim said, "did you think that you'd come to Salt Fork for one week and solve this case?"

"When you say it like that it sounds delusional." Judith stared at her hands again.

"You've done everything you can for now. But I can't arrest Granger because you had some visions about him. Do I think he's guilty? Yes. But I need to have evidence that will be admissible in court."

"I should have focused on finding out where he put her body," Judith said. "I was so focused on piecing together what happened leading up to her death, and now I can't get anything. It's like Autumn's just gone, like she decided I wasn't the right person for the job after all."

"I'll keep working on it," Tim said. "I'll question Granger, question his friends, ask around to see if anyone remembers him mentioning anything suspicious relating to Autumn's disappearance. I'll keep an eye on him, a close eye. And if I catch him peddling drugs again, I'll do my best to make sure he gets put away for as long as possible. It's not a murder charge, but he'll be off the streets. I'll keep you updated on any breakthroughs."

"I appreciate that." Judith dropped her eyes and plucked at a wrinkle in her sweatpants. "I know that's not standard procedure for someone in my position."

"I'll just consider you a volunteer cold case investigator," Tim said as he stood. "Nothing unusual or kooky about that."

A twinge of satisfaction flickered through Tim as another smile poked through the cracks of Judith's glare. "I don't appreciate your continued use of *kooky*."

Tim walked the few steps to the motel room door, the bag of remaining donuts swinging by his hip. "I never thought I'd take a psychic seriously, but you're something else."

He opened the door and stepped out into the chilly evening, but Judith held the door open.

"You do take me seriously?" she said, her voice quiet.

"I don't really have a choice. You barged into my office, started spouting off statistics, and ended up being right about all kinds of stuff you shouldn't have known. So yeah, I do."

It had crept up on him slowly, steadily, until it took him by surprise – but Tim didn't know quite what to make of the disappointment that nagged within him at the thought that tomorrow morning Judith wouldn't throw open his office door demanding information or permission to use the copier.

Tim shrugged his jacket a little tighter against a gust of wind. "If there's a way to prove what happened that night, then we'll find it." Waving, he stepped away toward his car. "See ya around, Psychic Lady."

"It's Judith. And goodbye, Sheriff."

"Goodbye, Judith. And you can call me Tim."

X

THE FOREST

Melissa Sloan had steered clear of lunchmeat, alcohol, and Oxy for five long months, but it was the littlest of the three, the pill, that she craved most.

Just this once, one pill as a celebration – that wouldn't be enough to give her baby the nasty withdrawals the narrow-eyed doctor had told her about, would it? He hadn't even asked if she took Oxy, just lowered his angry, suspicious eyebrows and told her off anyway.

But surely one pill, just tonight, wouldn't be enough to hurt the baby. She'd kept away from Oxy for so long, and Granger had suggested, actually suggested, that they celebrate.

All those months of worrying and wearing baggy shirts and hoping he wouldn't see the little, growing swell of her belly, of practicing the words in her head: *Not this one. I'm keeping this baby, with or without you.*

And after all those long, anxious months, tonight when the words spilled out of her, he hadn't pushed back with his quick-tongued arguing. He hadn't threatened to leave. He'd just sat, silent, staring into space past her, through her. Then, finally, with his lopsided grin, he'd said they oughta celebrate.

Just one pill, that was all he'd asked. One pill from his friend in the winding hollers up above town. One pill wouldn't hurt baby. Would it?

Melissa glanced over at Granger, one hand on the wheel and his elbow leaning out the open window, the dim light of the dashboard glowing on his face. The heavy, fragrant mountain air of the cool June night billowed in gusts, tossing his hair against his forehead.

There would be no drive to Virginia this time, no pills or procedures to make baby go away so that its father would stay. They'd be a family. Finally, a family.

Up above the streetlights of Salt Fork, the mountain road was bumpy and pitch black. Darkness grasped at them, encroaching on the golden shafts of their headlights.

"What friend did you say this was?" she asked.

"Robby. You remember Robby, dontcha, way up in the hollers? Been supplyin' me for a couple months since that sheriff's started breathin' down my neck."

"Didn't know Robby had a place up here. We gonna get there soon?"

"In a bit."

The blackness, thick and solid as a living thing in the cloudy starless night and the dense forest, pressed close as they wound up and up along the rugged trail. Melissa lurched with the truck, a rolling wave of nausea welling within her, and she laid her hand against her stomach and the little fluttering kicks inside.

Granger had made it clear, years ago, that he wanted no part in raising a family. And when precautions had failed and her heart had swelled and she'd begged to keep that first little baby, Granger again had made it clear.

But this time, when she hadn't begged, when she'd been the one to make it clear – that she would choose this baby over him if she had to, he'd given in. Like she always knew he would, someday. Finally, a family.

This change of heart, it was worth celebrating, just like Granger said. One pill wouldn't hurt.

The jostling truck rumbled to a halt, and Granger pulled the keys out of the ignition, plunging them into utter, wild darkness.

Melissa's body tensed with a primal fear. Then, with a click, a beam of yellow light lit up the cabin of the truck.

"Gotta walk the rest of the way," Granger said, opening the door. "Robby's house is real remote. Even that sheriff don't know nothin' 'bout it."

"There ain't nothin' out here but woods." Melissa clutched the door handle.

"Just a little farther, baby. Right up the hill. Then we can have one last big night before we got all them responsibilities."

The honeyed light stretched Granger's lopsided grin, distorting it with shadows. That grin – she'd given so much, again and again, clawing out the insides of herself to offer them up, hoping his smile would be aimed at her this time.

Sometimes it was. But she could never be sure about the next one.

Melissa tugged the truck door open and stepped down into the blackness.

Clutching Granger's arm, she followed him step by wheezing step up the tree-crowded slope, brambles scratching her ankles and catching on her jeans. The yellowed flashlight shone just enough to keep them moving forward, slowly, up the mountain, tracing the rambling line of what looked to be little more than a deer trail through the forest.

Sweat trickled, cold and trembling, down Melissa's spine. One hit, that's all - one pill. Granger wanted to celebrate. He was happy about baby, about her – she should encourage that however she could. Even if it meant stumbling up a mountain in the dead of night, the rest of Salt Fork long since asleep.

They hadn't even left the house until almost midnight. It had to be nearing one in the morning now.

Her doctor's eyes, slitted with judgment, and the tiny spikes of the fast-pattering heartbeat inside her pushed into her thoughts until suddenly she didn't see the yellow circle of light guiding her steps, didn't feel the thick press of forest. She saw only the grainy gray image she'd hidden away in her wallet, the tiny mouth already sucking a thumb.

"I don't wanna do this no more." Melissa stopped, tugging on Granger's arm. "I don't want one last hit. I been tryin' so hard not to take any pills, and I don't wanna fall off the wagon now."

"We're almost there, Mel. Don't be like this."

"It could give the baby withdrawals. My doctor said –"

"That's fine. You don't gotta have none. But I still want some, and Robby's got my stash." Granger pushed forward again, pulling Melissa along.

Melissa bit her lip and trailed a few steps behind as he kept moving, his hand clutching her arm. Granger sped up, shoving through underbrush.

"I can't go this fast," Melissa said. Somewhere deep within her, a memory stirred, a vague sensation she couldn't suss out. "I can't hike like this no more."

"We're gonna be there in just a bit. Almost there."

Melissa gasped for air, her lungs crowded by her growing belly as she struggled after Granger. They'd come up in the mountains plenty of times before – her and Granger, Autumn and Stewart and other tagalong friends. Daring each other to pry away a board and sneak into the old, closed up mine entrances scattered and hidden deep in the hollers. Kid stuff, stupid and dangerous and fun, if nobody got too cocky.

They'd been up here before.

A sudden fear, deep and visceral and overpowering, roiled within her, and she pulled her arm away.

"Robby don't have no house up here."

"He just ain't talked to you about it." Granger turned toward her, but the beam of the flashlight still pointed forward, into the silent woods. "You think he'd go around tellin' you and your blabbermouth 'bout where he hides out from the sheriff?"

"You ain't never mentioned it before tonight."

"He's my friend. Didn't see a need to bring it up."

Granger seized Melissa's elbow and pulled her along behind the frenetic yellow beam that stabbed into the blackness.

Her body went cold and clammy, terror freezing over her skin as she plodded up the mountain, dragged along by Granger.

Between the tramping of their feet in the rotting leaves, with each step Granger took there was a faint, muffled jingle.

The keys.

Melissa's teeth chattered, but memories flooded her mind. The warped wood that marked the abandoned mines, the earth-deep darkness, the stale and musty air that had always repulsed her. A feral instinct crept into her veins, a hideous suspicion she wouldn't name.

Granger's foot caught in a tangle of undergrowth, and he paused to shake it free.

Melissa yanked her arm from his grip and with a frantic swipe shoved her hand into his pocket.

Her fingers closed around the jagged metal of the keys. Pulling them free, she turned and staggered in a clumsy run down the hill, straining her eyes against the crushing darkness.

Where was the truck?

Her shoulder slammed against a tree, and she threw her hands out in front of her, scrabbling for a route through the black night.

Granger didn't yell, didn't scream at her to stop.

At first there was only the rapid, panicked crunching of her feet in the dead leaves, the gasping of her breath, and the pounding of her heart, an island of noise in the still, silent forest.

Then, behind her, she heard footsteps sliding down the mountain, and a flashlight beam lit her from behind, throwing her shadow across the trees.

Smothering a shriek, Melissa darted forward, fighting against the steep gravity of the slope, against the roots that snatched at her feet, against the branches that slapped at her arms.

Behind her came thundering footsteps and heavy, angry breaths.

Her thoughts broke –

There was no plan.

Only the keys she clutched in her shaking hand and the enveloping darkness and her stabbing lungs and her swollen belly – no, she couldn't fall, couldn't land on her stomach, she had to be careful. But he was closer now, was pounding down the mountain toward her, and she couldn't see the truck, couldn't see the trees that sprang at her, could only hear him and his furious, growling breath –

A strong hand snatched a handful of Melissa's hair.

XI

THE SHAFT

Judith woke with a scream clawing her throat. She bolted upright, thrashing her legs free of her tangled, sweat-soaked sheets.

Grabbing for her bedside lamp, she missed and knocked it over with a dull thump. She snatched her phone instead, yanked it free of its charger, turned on the flashlight, and shone it around her still, quiet room.

Her breaths coming in ragged gasps, she checked the time.

10:03pm.

She hadn't been asleep for long, hardly more than thirty minutes.

It was as though Autumn had been lying in wait, ready to pounce into her dreams.

With shaking hands, Judith dialed.

Tim answered on the second ring. "Well, hello." His voice was relaxed, untired, as though he was going about the normal course of his evening, sleep still a distant reality. "I didn't expect to hear from you this time of night."

"Granger's going to kill Melissa. You need to go to his house. They might still be there, but he's taking her up in the mountains –"

"Hang on." The smile was gone from his voice, but still he spoke slowly. "Take a breath, slow down, and tell me what happened."

"I saw it. In a vision. I saw him take Melissa up into the mountains, by an old mine –" Squeezing her hand into a fist, Judith stabbed her palm with her fingernails and forced a breath into her lungs. "I don't know if it's happening now, or if it's going to happen, or if she's already –" She swallowed the words, her throat suddenly tight.

"I'll do a drive-by." Like an inverse function undoing the jagged shrillness of her voice, Tim's tone went down, smoother and lower and calmer. "I'll go by their house and see if they're there, if anything's suspicious."

"I'm coming." Judith scrambled out of bed, righted her bedside lamp, and snatched mismatched clothing from her closet.

"You're two hours away. Just try to go to sleep and get some rest. Or, if you can't sleep, watch some TV or something. I'll call you and let you know what I see when I get there."

"I'm coming." Judith yanked her legs through her jeans and pulled a sweatshirt over her pajama shirt.

"Judith –"

"He took her up in the mountains, where there are no houses and no roads. He parked his car in the woods and started walking. There is no way you'll be able to find them without me."

"You don't sound like you're in any state to drive for two hours in the dark."

"I'm coming." Judith hung up the phone. Running out of her bedroom and through her darkened house, she snatched her keys and purse from their respective hooks, threw open the front door, and darted out into the night.

⋯

The clustered lights of downtown Lexington had given way to the duller glow of nighttime suburbia by the time Judith's phone rang.

"They're at the house," Tim said. "I can see their silhouettes through the window."

"Then it hasn't happened yet." The knot in Judith's chest released, just slightly. She sped down the quiet highway, southeast toward Salt Fork. "But he's planning it."

"I'll stay and keep an eye on the house for a while."

Judith clutched the steering wheel tighter. "I'm not making this up."

"I don't think you are."

"You sound skeptical."

"Not skeptical of *you*," Tim said, and in the crackle of his phone's spotty reception, Judith thought she detected a stifled sigh. "You said your visions aren't always completely accurate. You were very upfront about your margin of error."

"I *saw* it. If it hasn't happened yet, it's going to. It was –" Judith faltered at the heat in her voice. Where was her notebook? Had she left it lying on her bedside table? Had she written down the vision or anything about it? Had she really let her objectivity evaporate at the first sign of danger? "It felt urgent. Imminent."

"Look, I'll stay as long as I can. But if I get called out for an emergency, I'm going to have to leave."

"Don't you have a deputy or someone who can stay and keep watch?"

Tim chuckled with an unconcealed sigh. "I'm supposed to. His wife had twins a while ago, then he hurt his back and has been out on short-term disability for a bit without a replacement. Small county problems. I can call him in an emergency, but –"

"He won't be very helpful if anything happens with Granger."

"Exactly. And, unless I know for sure that there's an emergency, I don't want to wake him up in the middle of the night if I don't have to."

"What about sheriffs in neighboring counties?"

"If this escalates to an emergency, then, sure, I can call them. But if I called them now and asked them to stake out a house in the middle of the night because my favorite psychic told me a crime was going to be committed, they'd chew my ear off."

"You can tell them my accuracy rate, and I'll email you my spreadsheets. There are several graphs. Some of them are slightly on the complex side, but there's a very clear, color-coded key –"

"Judith, even with all the spreadsheets in the world, if I mention the word *psychic* to Sheriff Quinn in Bayton County, there's no way he's going to leave his house to drive all the way out here."

Judith pressed harder on the gas, her stomach growing hot with anxious rage.

"I'll keep an eye on them," Tim said, his voice reclaiming the hint of a smile. "Just don't drive like a maniac, please. If you're going to insist on coming, then stay safe and get here in one piece. I'll call you if anything changes."

Again, Judith hung up the phone.

The city lights grew sparser, the cloudy night swallowing the moon and stars, shrouding the sky in blackness.

It hadn't been just a dream. It hadn't. The darkness had been too intense, the evil too visceral. There had been intent – an old mine, its shaft dropping deep into the mountainside – and there had been fear too – a panicked, twisted fear, writhing through the vision like a sickness.

But what if it wasn't tonight?

What if she drove two hours, forced Tim to stake out Granger's house all night – all for nothing? And then, on another dark night, Granger killed Melissa in silence, in secret, and she disappeared without a trace, just like Autumn.

What if, yet again, Judith knew what had happened, but couldn't prove it?

...

Gas station coffee burned Judith's tongue but kept her eyes propped open through miles and miles of treacherous, winding roads.

Almost there, she was almost there.

Her phone rang again, lighting up the dashboard of her car and startling her from her thoughts.

"Hello?"

"Tell me everything you saw in your vision." Tim's voice was still low, still slow, but there was a tightness now, a coiled intensity that sent a hot jolt of fear crackling down Judith's spine.

"What happened?"

"I got a call. A scuffle in a bar. Everyone had cooled off by the time I got there, but I was gone for about thirty minutes."

Her fear turned cold, chilling Judith's skin. "Where's Granger?"

"The house is dark, and the truck is gone."

"No."

"I knocked on the door, and no one answered."

Judith drove faster. She whirled back through what she could remember of the vision, the nightmare. Mountain road, thick forest, pressing darkness, the warped boards blocking an old mine shaft. Murder, pulsing in a feverish heartbeat.

"He's going to dump her body in an abandoned mine shaft," she said.

"Did you see any identifying markers? Anything that could indicate where it is?"

"How many abandoned mines are there near Salt Fork?"

"This is coal country, has been for two hundred years. There are abandoned mines all over these mountains. Some of them are so old we don't even have records for them."

"I'm almost there." Judith sped up, flying around bends in the road. "I can help once I'm there. Just wait for me."

...

Tim was pacing beside his sheriff's car when Judith pulled up outside Granger and Melissa's run-down house, with its overgrown lawn and white vinyl siding.

Judith sprang out of her car and locked the door with a beep. "I need you to drive where I tell you to."

"Drive where?"

"And I need you to be quiet for a minute. Please."

Closing her eyes, Judith pressed her palms together and held her hands out in front of her. *Granger – where did you go?*

Calming her anxious breaths, Judith turned in a slow circle, tuning her thoughts and sensations on Granger, on whatever trail he'd left behind.

Judith's pounding heartbeat thudded, but as her breathing quieted, her other senses came to life.

Her fingertips dipped suddenly with a strange gravity, and Judith opened her eyes. "That way." She pointed into the distance, where the black mountains were indistinguishable from the starless sky.

Judith pulled on the passenger's side handle of the sheriff's car, but it didn't budge. Yanking his keys from his pocket, Tim unlocked the doors and slid into the driver's seat.

"Do you know a road that gets up to the mountains that way?" Judith said, climbing into the car.

"Don't know that I'd call it a road." Tim swung the car around and sped out of the small neighborhood toward the looming dark of the hills. "What was that you did just now, back there?"

"Dowsing."

"Excuse me?"

"Dowsing."

"Dousing? Like dumping water on somebody?"

"No," Judith said. "The *s* is voiced, like a *z*. Dowsing. It's a way to find things."

"Do you do that often?"

"Only when I'm looking for misplaced keys or my phone."

Tim was silent for a moment. "This is a little different."

"I know." A sharp note stabbed into Judith's voice, and she rubbed her hands on her knees.

The mountains and the darkness and Melissa and the baby and Granger – Judith had seen the bloodstained thoughts, felt the strangled, distorted rage and fear, the savage, discordant violence.

Judith pressed her hands together again, holding them out in front of her. "This way. Keep going this way."

...

The road turned to dirt, then to the bone-shaking jostle of land not meant for vehicles. Tim's car struggled and groaned its way up the claustrophobic hillside, the trees hemming them in, nearly blocking their path.

Judith bit her lip and glanced again at the clock.

12:59am.

"We won't be able to drive much further," Tim said, the car's dashboard lighting up his grim face.

"They're close," Judith whispered. "I think."

A shiver rolled through her. What if she was wrong? What if they were on another mountainside, beside a different mine –

Another body they'd never find –

"Wait." Tim slowed the car and pointed straight ahead. "Look at that."

Judith squinted through the darkness and the glare of the car's headlights, and gasped.

There, in the bright yellow glow of the car's light, was Granger's dark red truck.

"I'm calling Sheriff Quinn." Tim pulled out his phone.

During his quick, hushed conversation, Judith closed her eyes and reached out for Granger, for Melissa, though she struggled to see or hear anything over her own thudding heartbeat.

"He's on his way. " Pulling out a flashlight, Tim turned off the engine, plunging them into dark silence. "Stay in the car."

"They hiked up the mountain. You won't be able to find them without me."

With a click, the white beam of a flashlight lit the car. "I won't take a civilian."

"You said I'm a volunteer cold case investigator."

"You're still a civilian. I won't take you into a dangerous situation." Tim reached for the door handle.

"Do you know where the mine shaft is?"

"No, but you can point me in the right direction, can't you?"

"It could be another mile up the mountain, and you could get turned around. If you don't have me with you, your chances of finding them are miniscule."

Tim let out a tight breath. The dead silence of the moonless woods stretched between them, filling the car.

Finally, he sighed. "Okay. Just hang on." Tim opened the car door and crept to the trunk. He returned and pushed a thick, heavy bundle toward Judith. "But you're wearing this. And if you hear or see anything, or if I tell you to – and I mean the moment I tell you to – drop to the ground and lie on your stomach. Got it?"

"Is this your only vest?"

"If you're coming, you're wearing it."

Judith slipped the dense vest over her head. She pulled on the straps to tighten them, but still it hung like a box on her torso. She pointed to the gaping armholes, too big for her. "I don't think Kevlar is intended to fit this way."

"It's still better than nothing."

Behind the stark beam of the flashlight, Tim pushed through the underbrush, following Judith's directions. She walked behind, trying to place her feet in the same places he did as she stepped into impenetrable darkness and squelching, rain-damp leaves.

Her foot caught on something in the blackness, and she pitched forward with a gasp. Tim jerked around and grabbed her arm, then released a breath of relief when the flashlight showed nothing more dangerous than a tangle of roots. "Try to stay close so you can see the light," he murmured. "We need to stay quiet. We going the right way?"

Judith held her hands out in front of her again, turning until they dipped just slightly toward the ground with a soft, unearthly tug.

"No." She pointed slightly to the right. "That way."

The inky night loomed around Judith on every side, closing in everywhere except for the little beam of light that illuminated the trees and the grasping bushes, casting an ambient glow on Tim's face, his smile vanished and his jaw tight.

Judith was acclimated to the ever-present hum of city traffic and electricity, and the silence of the forest was thick, eerie, foreign to her ears. Their cautious footsteps were the only noise in the unsettling quiet, as though even the owls and deer and bats were hiding from the depths of the starless darkness.

Somewhere in the distance came the whisper of rustling leaves. The black night amplified every sound, warping it to monstrous intensity.

Icy fear prickled over Judith's skin. What was she doing here? She was a software developer from the city. She had no place here in the haunting stillness, stalking a murderer.

A wailing shriek stabbed through the dark silence. Its strange echo lingered in the blackness, somewhere just up the hill.

Tim bolted into the forest, his hand moving to his gun.

As her only source of light disappeared into the dense black woods, Judith's lungs clenched inward, and her throat tightened. Stumbling, she staggered through the trees after Tim.

The wail cut short, and a new sound grew louder as Judith scrambled up the steep slope.

Whimpering sobs, barely audible.

Tim crouched on the hillside, holding the flashlight low to conceal its beam. At a sharp gesture from Tim, Judith dropped to her stomach on the damp earth.

Tim crept forward, flashlight in one hand, his gun clutched in the other.

There it was – a cave. The mine entrance, its boards loose and broken and warped with age.

The suffocating, sickly-sweet reek of decaying leaves, so close to Judith's face, pushed itself ever closer in the utter darkness.

Darting forward into the tunnel, Tim disappeared from sight, but his voice bounded off the stony cavern. "Sheriff! Put your hands in the air!"

Judith heard him now, the soldier. A sharp-edged likeness of the man who'd eaten ice cream and laughed while rocking a rope bridge.

Closing her eyes, Judith quieted her breath, trying not to smell the leaf corpses around and beneath her, squirming their scent down her nose and throat.

Granger, Melissa, Tim –

Color and sound burst into Judith's mind, pulsating with dread.

Tim, gun drawn, flashlight pinned on Granger.

Granger, the barrel of his gun on Melissa's stomach.

Melissa, body racked with sobs, frozen between fear and frenzy.

Rage lashing out from Granger like tongues of flame, indiscriminate – the poisoned spawn of a hateful man.

A familiar icy shiver rolled through Judith, her fingertips going numb. Something – something strong and dark and desperate – pushed into her vision, and the image stuttered, speeding up like a film reel. Then it stopped, a snapshot –

Melissa on the ground, scarlet splattered in the heart of the mountain.

No – it wasn't real. No one had pulled a trigger yet.

Judith clenched her shaking hands, shoving back against the force hijacking her vision.

In a whirl, the strange force vanished, and the image in Judith's mind cleared again.

Tim speaking, his voice muffled as though underwater.

Granger, gun still pushing against Melissa, backing deeper into the tunnel.

Twisted fear, knotted and sharp as barbed wire, winding around Granger, stabbing into him and drawing out ichor, black and thick and guilty – his father's, and his, and now the same sickened, cursed blood preparing to force itself on the world again.

The poisoned spawn of a hateful man.

Judith's eyes flew open.

Whatever Tim was saying, it wasn't working.

The chill came again like a prodding, but Judith pressed herself harder against the damp ground.

She was supposed to stay here. That was the plan. She'd done what she could; anything else would make her a liability, a danger to herself, to Tim, to Melissa.

Cold enveloped her, and Judith reflexively squinted through the inky blackness for Autumn. But she saw nothing.

Ahead of her came the muffled rumble of raised voices. They couldn't be too far inside the cave.

Again an image forced into Judith's mind – *the flash of a gun, lightning in the stony tunnel, a body falling in a spray of blood.*

Scrambling to her feet, Judith clawed up the last slope of the hillside, the voices rising as she went.

She crested the hill and crept through the darkness toward the hole that stabbed into the bowels of the mountain, lit from inside with the dim glow of a flashlight bouncing off the stone walls.

"Sheriff, you come any closer, an' I pull this trigger right now!" Granger's voice was loud and ragged, panicking and furious, a dangerous combination.

Judith dropped to her stomach again, and a cascade of pebbles shook loose beneath her, rolling and clinking against each other down the slope.

"Who's out there?" Granger's voice came again.

Judith's breath strangled in her throat. From the ground, she could see the beam of Tim's flashlight in the cave – Granger's rabid fury, Melissa's tear-stained face.

In the quivering light, Granger's frantic eyes searched outside the mouth of the cave, distracted for a moment from Tim and his gun.

He stared past Tim, past the tunnel, past Judith huddling on the ground, out toward the still, black woods.

An icy gust whooshed past Judith, raising the hairs along her arm.

A hum like the droning of wasps filled Judith's ears, and suddenly Granger's face changed.

His eyes widened, his mouth dropping open.

He stumbled back from Melissa in a clawing panic, his mouth rounded in a scream Judith couldn't hear over the noise that flooded her mind. Granger fled, staggering further into the tunnel, outside the reach of Tim's flashlight.

Tim rushed forward, pushing Melissa toward the mouth of the tunnel before pursuing Granger deeper into the mine.

The droning suddenly stopped, leaving Judith's ears ringing.

Tim's voice burst like gunfire into the night. "Stop! Granger, stop!"

Granger's feral scream sliced through the forest. Echoing, tumbling, growing distant fast – too fast.

Then, sudden as a hammer strike, the mountain was silent.

Tim – where was Tim?

Her legs shaking, Judith crawled forward, following the sound of Melissa's sobs.

The tunnel walls were smooth gray stone interspersed with rotten wooden beams, an old wound in the mountain. In the faint light that ricocheted off the walls, Melissa lay curled on the ground, her arms cradling her stomach.

Judith crept closer to Melissa and strained her eyes for a glimpse of Tim in the distance.

Down the tunnel, further into the swallowing darkness, Tim stood with his flashlight at the edge of a black pit, a deep hole bored into the earth, and looked down, his shoulders slumped.

"Melissa?" Crouching beside her, Judith tried to think of what Constance would do but came up blank. Constance had never tracked a murderer and his intended victim into a coal mine. And, as far as Judith knew, Constance had never had to comfort someone moments after they had cheated death –

Melissa threw her arms around Judith's shoulders, yanking Judith down to the ground with her, and held tight, her sobs shaking them both and soaking into Judith's sweatshirt.

Judith tensed. Raising one hand, she patted Melissa's shoulder.

Footsteps, slow and heavy, came toward them, and through the dimness Judith's eyes caught Tim's.

He looked back toward the gaping hole of the mine shaft and shook his head.

Cold wind rushed again past Judith, gushing out of the cave into the forest, and warmth snuck back into the quiet June night.

XII

THE GOODBYE
(REPRISE)

The vines snaking up the walls of the Mitchell house had shed the dull bronze of fading winter for the rich, flowering green of early summer.

In the balmy, late afternoon warmth, Judith hesitated on the sidewalk, crossing her arms over the *Welcome to Kentucky!* t-shirt she'd bought at the McFerrin gas station to replace her pajama shirt and sweatshirt, which were stale with sweat and stained by dirt and dead leaves. The few hours heavy sleep she'd gotten in McFerrin's motel were enough to keep her on her feet, but her body was sapped, depleted in the aftermath of the jagged fear, the midnight chase up the mountains, the echoes of Granger's screams plummeting into the earth –

Judith stabbed her fingernails into her arm and shook her head, pushing the memories away, holding them at arm's length.

She had one more thing to do before she left Salt Fork.

As she took a breath to steel herself, behind her came the crunch of tires and the creak of a car door opening.

"Judith?"

Turning, Judith came face to face with Anna May Schneider, her round eyes wide and sheepish.

Anna May shut the minivan door and fiddled with the hem of her shirt. "Are you going inside?"

"I'd like to do a debrief of the case," Judith said. "I realize I am no longer working for you, but given recent events –"

"No, it's fine. You can – I'm –" Anna May trailed off, her eyes searching for words in the house, the sky, the sidewalk. "Why don't we go in?"

Judith followed Anna May up the path, overgrown by a lawn that was more weeds than grass. When they reached the porch, Anna May stopped and stood rooted to the warped wooden planks, her eyes on the window.

Frowning, Judith followed Anna May's gaze.

The window opened onto an alcove in the living room, where Rock and Cindy Mitchell sat, their fingers intertwined and knuckles resting on the faded wood of the table. The television was black and silent.

"Is something wrong?" Judith whispered.

Anna May's eyes glistened in the golden afternoon sunlight, and her voice was thick. "I don't remember the last time I saw them do that."

Judith waited, shifting her weight between her feet, until Anna May finally stepped forward and rang the doorbell.

From inside came the scrape of chairs, the shuffling of feet, and Cindy opened the door.

But the Cindy in the doorway was not the gray, deflated woman of months before. Like color returning to a withered flower, her gray curls were not so limp, her skin not so sallow. There was a hint of light in her eyes, a slight pink in her cheeks.

Without a word, she stepped back, making way for them to enter.

When Judith's gaze met Rock's in the sun-dappled living room, the softness in his eyes soured. Slapping his baseball cap onto his head, he stood, squeezed Cindy's hand, and left through the open front door.

Cindy wrapped Anna May in an embrace that lasted long enough to twist Judith's stomach into awkward knots. Pulling back, Cindy rubbed Anna May's shoulders. "Why don't you make some coffee. I wanna talk to Miss Temple here."

Her body tight with uncertainty, Judith followed Cindy through the house and out the back door to the yard, where just beyond the fence the mountains rose in sun-rich green. Cindy sank onto on a worn patio swing.

Judith hesitated, then reached for a plastic lawn chair. With a shake of her head, Cindy patted the cushion beside her.

Perching on the edge of the swing, Judith wove her fingers together and clutched her knees, waiting.

Cindy pushed the swing back and forth, back and forth, her eyes on the trees and their golden-green leaves.

"News travels fast here," Cindy said at last.

"I assume you're referring to Granger."

"Sheriff came by not too long before you got here, but we'd already heard all about it from the neighbors." With her toes, Cindy kept moving the swing back and forth, back and forth. "There're rumors goin' around that a psychic lady called the sheriff'n told him Granger was about to kill little Melissa Sloan. Judgin' by the dirt stains on your jeans, I'm guessin' that's true. You drove all the way down here last night, didn'tcha?"

"That's correct." Judith rubbed at the stubborn brown stains on her jeans and cleared her throat. "I have a theory."

"A theory? And what is it you got a theory about?"

"About you," Judith said. "I think you have some very strong psychic functioning, and that's what prevented me from doing my readings around you."

A small smile snuck onto Cindy's face. "When I was a little girl, I'd sometimes see things other people couldn't see, know things other people didn't know, things I had no way of knowin'. Ignored it, mostly, when I got older."

"It felt like you were blocking me. Like radio interference."

"Mighta been somethin' like that. I don't rightly know."

Judith studied her ruined shoes. "You saw Autumn, didn't you?"

The swing kept up its steady rhythm – back and forth, back and forth.

"You ain't got no idea what it's like," Cindy said, her voice as quiet and constant as the back and forth, back and forth of the patio swing, "knowin' your baby's dead and gone, and havin' to see her day after day, standin' there all bloody, covered in dirt. She never said nothin', just stood in corners, on the edge of crowds. She was tryin'a tell me somethin', but I never could figure out what. I couldn't live with it. Blocked her out, pushed her away – I guess that's what I did. Whatever it was that I did, it was only to keep me from dyin' inside."

The sterile, curated words of Judith's burgeoning theories – psychic functioning, medium, buffer, interference, Purgatory – strained for release, but she held them in check. She didn't need to let them loose, not now. It was a hard, slow-learned lesson for her, that not everything had to be said.

"I got some theories too." Cindy gave a heavy sigh. "My baby couldn't get to me, so she got to you, when it mattered. I think she knew; I think she saw what Granger was fixin' to do. What happened to her, she didn't want it happenin' again. And she found a way. My baby always found a way."

Cindy lapsed into silence, filled only by the creak of the old swing.

As the sun drifted closer to the tops of the trees along the mountain ridge, Judith's fingertips started to tingle, and she stilled. Cindy gasped, and Judith raised her eyes.

There in the yard, amid the golden sunlight and the soft breeze, was Autumn.

Her long, dark hair lay in wisps over her shoulders, and a bright sundress fluttered about her. In her arms, resting on her hip, was a dark-haired girl with tight black curls and wide green eyes, her little fingers clutching the fabric of Autumn's dress.

Autumn smiled and pressed her cheek against the little girl's forehead.

With a last look that settled over Cindy and Judith with the warmth of the afternoon sunshine, Autumn, holding her green-eyed little girl, turned and moved with slow, smooth steps toward the fence.

She opened the gate, closed it behind her, latched it.

Then, following the gentle billows of the wildflowers, Autumn and her daughter traveled up the hill, through the glow of approaching evening and into the deep green of the mountain forest.

...

The evenings were long now, with daylight holding tight to the earth even into the nighttime hours. There would still be plenty of sunlight left for the two hours back to Lexington.

Judith checked her phone again as if she somehow could have missed Tim's call in the past thirty seconds.

She wouldn't call him a second time. Two calls would be excessive.

But it didn't seem right, even to her, to leave McFerrin without saying goodbye.

The previous night, sitting for what had felt like hours in the flashes of red and blue that lit the forest, listening to the murmur of Tim's voice and the gruff bluster of Sheriff Quinn as the two sheriffs called and woke people across both their counties – paramedics for Melissa, officers from McFerrin township's tiny police force, a recovery team to rappel into the mine shaft – she and Tim hadn't had a chance to exchange another word.

Judith hated loose ends, unanswered questions.

But, in addition to Tim, there was something else niggling at Judith, itching at her.

She had to try, just once before she left. Just to answer her own questions.

Holding her clasped hands in front of her, Judith closed her eyes.

Autumn, where are you?

She waited, turning slowly, listening.

A gentle tug on her fingertips pointed her north, and Judith started up her car, pulling onto the country road crowded by trees as steep and close as the arches of a summer-green Gothic cathedral.

On the quiet roads, every now and then Judith stopped, closing her eyes, holding out her hands, letting the tug guide her. It led her onto the northern mountain road. The same general direction as Lexington, she reminded herself. This was little more than a detour.

In the mountains above Salt Fork, a sign boasted a scenic overlook, and the pull at her fingertips tugged harder.

Judith steered her car off the road onto the wide gravel parking area of the overlook. A black SUV was parked beside the sign as well, its windows too dark to see if it was empty. Climbing out of her car, Judith followed the marked trail away from the street and through the trees.

Surely Granger hadn't hidden Autumn's body here, so close to the road.

Judith's winding thoughts stopped cold when she stepped through a clutch of trees onto a narrow path bounded by a crumbling rock wall, and stood looking directly at Tim Morrissey.

Tim turned as she approached, and his tired smile made the sunlight too warm and gave Judith a sudden urge to flee back to her car.

"What're you doing all the way up here?" Tim's hat, the ridiculous hat that made him look even taller than nature made him to be, was nowhere in sight, though his hair still bore its dent.

"I'm not following you," Judith said. "I called. To say goodbye. But I didn't know you were here."

With a gentle chuckle, Tim leaned against the wall and pointed to the holler below, drenched with the lush colors of a lingering golden sunlight. "The view used to be a lot better. But it's still a sight to see."

Judith took a few hesitant steps forward and peeked over the edge of the rock wall, which appeared to be the only barrier preventing them from tumbling over a sheer, rocky cliff into the valley.

Down below them, amid the thick green trees and the rolling hills that stretched for miles, was a cluster of rectangular gray buildings and circular pools of dark blue water. A water treatment plant.

"I was looking for Autumn," Judith whispered.

Tim shrugged as though to push away a shiver. "Looking for Autumn?"

"All day, I just couldn't get it out of my mind. The whole time I was investigating, I was so focused on finding her killer that I didn't leave myself time to try to find her body. That's how I ended up here. I was dowsing."

"You've gotta be kidding me."

"I generally don't *kid*."

Tim chuckled again and shook his head. "I'll give you one guess as to what I'm doing here."

"I don't like guessing games. I prefer logic puzzles in which I have all the available information in front of me." Judith leaned back from the wall, away from the cliff and the trees below as distant as fluffy green clouds. "Are you looking for Autumn too?"

"Technically I took today off. Needed some beauty sleep. But a thought's been bugging me all afternoon – there were no other bodies, at least none they could find, in that mine shaft, only Granger's. If Granger hadn't dumped Autumn in that shaft, then where was she? And if he already had a body-hiding spot that had evaded law enforcement for two decades, why switch and try to take Melissa someplace new?"

Tim turned around, lounging his back and elbows along the wall. "So I started wondering about all the reasons why he might have gone looking for a new place. What if his old spot was compromised? That made me think about what's been built in the hollers in the past twenty years. Mind you, not many new things have been built out here aside from a hospital or two. But about five years ago the county stuck this thing, this water treatment plant, up here in the hills where there used to be nothing but trees and the occasional hunting cabin. When they put that place in, there would have been bulldozers and excavators all over the mountain that wouldn't have noticed, let alone stopped to look at, some mostly-decomposed bones."

"You got all that from thinking about it for an afternoon?"

Tim raised an eyebrow and smiled. "You got here from following a ghost pulling on your fingers?"

"That's not an accurate representation of how dowsing works."

Tim, seeming perfectly at ease while leaning against a dubious wall over a rocky cliff, turned toward the valley again and looked down at the concrete, the sharp angles, the ponds in their precise, equidistant circles. "I just wanted to come up here and see it for myself, see if it felt right."

"You say things just *feel right* as though the sensation is objective fact," Judith said. "As evidence, it's highly suspect."

A laugh burst from Tim, loud and open and surprising, and despite her best efforts and a surge of defensiveness, Judith caught herself smiling.

"Things don't *feel right* or *feel wrong* to me," Judith continued over Tim's laughter. "If I physically see something in front of me, then I know it's there, and if I have a vision of something, then I know there's at least some truth to it, even if it's more abstract than I would prefer. But *feeling* has nothing to do with it, and my spreadsheets can corroborate what I'm saying."

"Every word out of your mouth is the opposite of every psychic stereotype I've ever heard."

"Thank you."

When Tim's chuckles subsided, he turned to Judith, a more somber note in his voice. "I forgot, I was going to mention – Melissa's gonna be going up to Lexington once the hospital discharges her."

"Lexington?"

"For rehab. Really, I think she mostly just needs a quiet place for a while."

Judith nodded, a sudden torrent of thoughts rushing through her mind.

Lexington. Anywhere in Lexington would put Melissa within half an hour of Judith's house. Would she be expected to visit Melissa? Bring food? God forbid – make small talk? Rehab and quiet – of course Judith wanted Melissa to have those things. But the thought of directionless chit chat with a relative stranger – particularly a relative stranger who was beholden to her – was enough to raise the tide of Judith's anxiety like seawater gushing over floodgates.

"–almost no way we'd get a warrant to tear up the plant looking for her body."

"Hm?" Judith started, suddenly aware that Tim was talking to her.

"I said it's going to be nigh on impossible to get a warrant that would let us search that plant for Autumn's body. We'd have to tear up the concrete; it'd be a mess. And we don't have any solid evidence that she's even there."

"I don't think Autumn cares if we find her."

"You get that feeling too?"

"It's not a feeling," Judith said. "I thought that was what she wanted, at first. It's how I perceived the first dream, the one that put me in touch with Anna May. But since then, the communications I've had from her dealt with finding and stopping Granger. She didn't seem to care whether or not I found her body."

"Still, it'd be good for her family, for their closure."

"I think they're doing all right," Judith said quietly.

Tim cocked his head at her, then nodded, turning his face back to the valley.

The rustle of the evening breeze through the leaves, the soft bleating of cicadas, the whisper of squirrels wrestling and racing through the tree branches – the rich sunset stillness stretched between them, and a strange, uncomfortable tugging stirred within Judith.

"I'd better get going," she said, stepping back from the wall. "I don't want to be driving in the dark."

Tim pushed himself off the wall as well, moving with her back down the narrow path to the road.

"Hey," Tim said, a step behind her. "I really am glad you came to Salt Fork. It's been a wild ride."

"When I accepted this job, I didn't expect a cold case to involve so much adrenaline."

"You handled yourself pretty well."

"As did you." Judith took a few more steps, then stopped. She turned around in the middle of the path. "But the next time you're confronting someone who has a gun, please wear your Kevlar."

"I don't usually have a civilian with me. That was an extenuating circumstance."

"Some studies report that law enforcement officers suffer fatal injuries at a rate almost four times higher than that of other occupations."

"Did you look that up today?" Tim said, and the smile that crept across his face sent a rush of irritation through Judith, along with another sensation that she definitely did not want to be dealing with on her way out of Salt Fork. "Are you *concerned?*"

"I was curious. About the statistics."

"If you say so."

"I do say so." Judith spun back around and hurried the last few steps to the road, where their cars sat undisturbed along the gravel shoulder.

As he emerged from the path, Tim held out his hand. "Let me know the next time you're in this neck of the woods. And I'll call you if I ever need a psychic."

Judith took his outstretched hand and shook it. "Southeast Kentucky isn't on the way to many places. I doubt I'll be in this neck of the woods *unless* you need a psychic."

The handshake stretched several seconds longer than the businesslike handshakes to which Judith was accustomed, and her face was hot and flushed in the gentle June evening.

She extricated her hand. "Well. Goodbye, then. Until you need a psychic."

"Can I give you a call the next time I pass through Lexington?"

"You – can. Yes. You can do that."

"Okay, then."

Tim's grin was infectious, and Judith turned away to hide her reddening face as she walked to her car.

"Drive safe," Tim said.

"Wear your Kevlar." Climbing into her car, Judith closed the door behind her.

Judith started her engine and pulled away from the scenic overlook, back onto the winding, tree-lined highway. When she glanced in her rearview mirror, there was Tim, leaning against his SUV and waving, a laugh in his eyes and the warm spring sunset slanting through the trees and puddling him in leaf-dappled gold.

Judith waved once, then turned her eyes back to the road ahead.

Acknowledgments

The bits and bobs that eventually would become *Down in the Holler* started floating around in my head several years before Judith and her story came to life in their first iteration as a serialized novella on Substack. When the time was finally right to bring *Down in the Holler* into the light, I was amazed and incredibly excited to find that my quirky paranormal mystery featuring a prickly, socially awkward psychic detective drew together a lovely cohort of Substack readers who were as invested in the story as I was.

To Judith's original, devoted readers - you know who you are - thank you from the bottom of my heart for your enthusiasm and encouragement. This book wouldn't exist without you!

Thank you to Jimmy Akin, Dom Bettinelli, and their podcast *Jimmy Akin's Mysterious World* for its balanced, clear-headed discussion of paranormal phenomena and psychic detectives. Jimmy Akin analyzes alleged psychic phenomena in several podcast episodes and provides information about the different types of reported phenomena, how real-life psychics cooperate with law enforcement, and how paranormal investigators approach their work. Much of my, and therefore Judith's, knowledge of paranormal terminology and categorization comes from this podcast, and I highly recommend it to anyone who is interested in learning more.

I need to give a very special thank you to Sara Dietz for helping me stay motivated to make this book a reality and for providing publishing expertise and an amazing cover design! She helped me push past my procrastination to bring Judith into print, which may never have happened without her help.

Thank you to my lovely sister and my dad, both of whom were Judith's first readers, before her story even made it to Substack. Thank you, forever and ever, to my husband, who spent innumerable Saturday mornings with the kids so that I could have a few hours to myself to write. And thank you to my kids, for (mostly) going easy on their dad on Saturday mornings, and for hugging me as if they hadn't seen me in months when I arrived home.

Bridget Riley lives in Oklahoma with her husband, three children, two cats, and a gentle giant of a dog. When not writing or wrangling young children, Bridget can be found baking sourdough or rereading Jane Austen and Dorothy Sayers.

To read more Judith Temple stories and other exclusive fiction, visit her newsletter, *Naptime Novelist*, on Substack!